Letters
From the
Horse Latitudes

For my esteemed and worthy
publisher, Judy Alter, without
whom this would not be!
All best and many thanks!
Charlie L. 10-12-94

Books by C. W. Smith

Novels

Thin Men of Haddam
Country Music
The Vestal Virgin Room
Buffalo Nickel

Nonfiction

Uncle Dad

LETTERS FROM THE

HORSE LATITUDES

SHORT FICTION BY
C. W. SMITH

Texas Christian University Press
Fort Worth

Acknowledgements

I would like to thank the National Endowment for the Arts for its support for this collection.
"The Plantation Club" originally appeared in *Southwest Review*. Winner of the John H. McGinnis Award for the best short fiction appearing in *SR*. Reprinted in *Southwest Fiction* (Bantam Books) and in *Hot and Cool: Jazz Short Stories* (Plume/Penguin).
"Tickler" was published in *American Literary Review*.
"A Letter From the Horse Latitudes" appeared in *The Missouri Review*.
"Tether" appeared in *Cimarron Review*.
"Witnesses" was published in *American Short Fiction*.
"Domestic Help" was published as "Fool and Pathfinder" in *Quartet*. Winner of the Frank O'Connor Memorial Award for the best short story appearing in the magazine.
"Child Guidance" appeared as "Henry: A Guide" in *Southwest Review*.
"The Man With Unusual Luck" was published in *Sunstone Review*.
"Hugo Molder and the Symbol of Displaced Persons Everywhere" appeared in *Focus: Media*.
"Western History" appeared in *New Mexico Humanities Review*.

Library of Congress Cataloging-in-Publication Data

Smith, C. W. (Charles William), 1940 –
   Letters from the horse latitudes : short fiction / C. W. Smith.
      p. cm.
   Contents: Tickler – The Plantation Club – Letter from the horse latitudes – Hugo Molder and the symbol of displaced persons everywhere – Western history – The man with unusual luck – Child guidance – Domestic help – Tether – Plane – Witness.
   ISBN 0 – 87565 – 131 – 3
   1. Southwestern States – Fiction. 2. Mexico – Fiction. I. Title.
PS3569.M516L48 1994
813'.54 – dc20
                                                    94 – 6505
                                                         CIP

Contents

To William and Helen
parents par excellence

Tickler

*S*oon as I signed my divorce papers, I thought of Waylan Kneu for the first time in decades. Waylan leased pinball machines and jukeboxes to taverns and dance halls; in a small New Mexico town divided distinctly between those who drank and danced and those who didn't, his "amusement" business gave him a roguish, disreputable air.

The Civil Air Patrol had an observation tower in the city park, and one Saturday morning I was alone there scanning the skies when Waylon's white-over-red El Camino pulled to the curb below. The El Camino, a low, swoop-backed pickup with a shallow bed, was a new model for Chevrolet then, and it always made me think of Las Vegas, though I'd never been there. (Darrell Sims's older brother called it a "cockwagon.")

Waylan got out and peered up at me, one hand shading his eyes. His hair was very black — he looked vaguely "Indian" — and he wore boots and a black leather vest over a pearl-button shirt. Standing in the bed of the pickup was a jukebox, all chrome and colored plastic and rounded comic corners. It and the truck together had the festive look of a parade entry.

"Say, Sport, you wanna earn some money?" he yelled up. "I got to take this juke to George's and I need a strong back to help me."

"Sure, Mr. Kneu!"

He was the only adult who nicknamed me; I was big for my age, but I was only fourteen, and the way he talked to me as an equal made me eager to please him. However, I still had fifteen minutes left on my duty watch. I wanted to ask him if he could wait, but no boy I knew would make such a request to an adult male. Reluctantly, I closed out the logbook with a vow to add fifteen minutes to my next watch and climbed down from the tower worrying that the Russians had been waiting for precisely such a small window of opportunity.

Waylan was smoking a Pall Mall; he carried the pack in a little pocket in the vest, and the red top stood vivid against the black leather. His face was pockmarked from old acne, but he was cowboy-handsome, and he grinned when he teased me or his wife or my mother, using his droll, whiskey-and-cigarette baritone. He had a laugh like a shotgun's pop, and he'd punctuate it by slapping whatever was close by with the fingers of one hand.

As we pulled away from the curb, he winked at me. "What do you do up there?"

"Watch for Russian planes." I blushed furiously; that he thought I'd be masturbating while on duty wounded my pride. "MIG 15s, TU 20s."

"Really?" he asked, deadpan. "You ever see any?"

"Not yet." But each time a Continental Airlines DC-3 or
a Piper Cub appeared on the horizon bound for our town's
one-runway airport, my hackles rose; I recorded each sight-
ing in the logbook, feeling like an Army Intelligence officer. People a lot older than I believed the Russians might
bomb the oil fields.

"What will you do if you see one?"

"Report it."

"How?"

"Run to the police station." I saw Boy Saves Town as a
headline and blushed again.

"I was Navy in the Big One, carrier duty in the Pacific."
He said this to mollify me, as if to compare our service, not
contrast it.

"Did you see any combat?"

"I wasn't no hero. I didn't much like being shot at, to
tell the truth." He chuckled and gave me a sly, sidelong
look. "What I liked was putting into port. Whew! I had
some good times!" He grinned at me, and I grinned back,
without understanding, in imitation.

George's had a large dance floor, and a band called The
Plowboys played there weekends. When we opened the rear
doors to carry the jukebox inside, the sunlight entered precisely three feet and stopped abruptly as if swallowed by a
black hole. The new jukebox was more bulky than heavy,
and we took it inside to a corner where the old one sat
dark. The place smelled of damp wood and stale beer. A
few ranch hands and oil-field roughnecks were talking quietly at the bar. The lighted neon signs over the bar —
Hamms, Pabst, Coors, Jax — looked exotic to me.

As soon as Waylan plugged the new box in, he flipped
through Kitty Wells, Carl Perkins, the Sons of the Pioneers,
Bob Wills, Lefty Frizell, Earnest Tubb, and punched a
number. While the tune played, he adjusted the sound with

knobs on the back. "Oh, I'm a honky-tonk man / And I
can't seem to stop. . . ."

Honky-tonk. That's where I am! I thought as I followed
Waylan to the bar. He ordered a Jax for himself, and the bar-
tender gave me a Coca-Cola in a bottle that might as well have
had a rubber nipple on it. While he and Waylan chatted, my
gaze wandered to the shuffleboard with its long, hooded lamp
hanging upside down like a feed trough, to the bottles sol-
diered behind the bar, to the tin-hatted roughnecks drinking
beer from cans and rolling their cigarettes. To my knowledge,
my father had never been in a honky-tonk; maybe he had, but
he'd never told me about it.

When Waylan's song ran out, a tin hat fed the machine a
nickel to play "Your Cheatin' Heart." Waylan said, "Give
this boy another soda." He went out to the pickup, came in
carrying a small carton, and vanished into the men's room.
I didn't want him to think I was lazy, so I chugged my second Coke and followed him.

Mounted on the wall was a long metal box; its face was
open, and Waylan was refilling it from the carton of pack-
aged condoms on the sink.

"Oops!" He grinned.

"I thought I'd help," I offered.

"Don't think your ma'd appreciate that much. Thanks
just the same. Speaking of her, I'd just as soon you didn't
say anything to your folks about this part of my business."

"Ok." I shrugged. "Sure." I wondered if I should leave,
but leaving might imply I'd caught him at something
shameful, and, also, now I was his accomplice. I was
awestruck to know something about my parents' friend
they didn't, and pleased that it was a secret between us.

He smiled and held up a package. "You know what these
are?"

"Sure. Rubbers."

"You know what people do with them?"

"Yeah. Sure."

He handed me a thin square packet wrapped in cellophane. "This is for prevention of disease," he said seriously, as if reading. "And also, you should use one if you get with a girl so you won't knock her up. You understand?" He squinted at me as if to assess my age, though he knew it. I suppose that, being childless, he had no clear notion of when a kid was ready for such information.

When I tried to hand it back, he waved me off with a grin. "That's a French tickler. Keep it for good luck."

"Thanks, Mr. Kneu." I gulped. A French tickler! The Holy Grail!

At home in my room, I put the packet in my wallet's "secret compartment." I was afraid to break open the package for fear of damaging the condom and had to be content to study the drawing on the wrapper: it depicted a rubber gizmo shaped like a pocket comb attached to the condom's tip. Schoolyard talk said the French tickler was like the legendary "Spanish fly" — both were guaranteed to make the most righteous virgin hysterical with lust. "French" coupled with "tickler" were words that would inflame any boy's imagination, and the name conjured up the old childhood chant: There's a place in France where the women wear no pants. . . .

These were years before sex education in the schools, before explicit magazines, films and books. I had been instructed in "the birds and the bees," but I hadn't quite connected "biological reproduction" with the sensations that swept over me when I looked at Daisy Mae, the Vargas calendar at the plumbing shop, the winged White Rock nymph, or the underwear models in the Sears catalog. I got all choked up, overheated. Swellings burgeoned up suddenly and unpredictably not only in my groin but also in my skull and my heart. I'd kissed several girls on the mouth, and on a recent church hay ride I had spent an hour working up to passing my hand quickly and lightly over the hump in Louise Bowen's blouse and finally did it. I did it very fast, but not even a lightning speed would have prevented me from vividly reliving time and again that millisecond of softness across my palm. Having the French tickler was like being given a souvenir to a World Wonder that I had not been to but had long been yearning to visit.

My parents had come to New Mexico from Tennessee; my father was an engineer with an oil company and my mother a legal secretary. They had attended Vanderbilt. They listened to Chopin and Beethoven and Glenn Miller, read *The New Yorker, Newsweek,* and *The Wall Street Journal.* My mother dabbled in watercolors and wrote poetry; my father smoked a pipe and attended church with unfailing regularity. I never heard them argue, and I never heard them curse. If there had been television in our town then, they would have watched only PBS or *The Hallmark Hall of Fame.*

Now it seems odd that they would have been friends with Waylan Kneu. He was different from the congregation who gathered at the Presbyterian potluck suppers, but I never questioned that then. I had a child's sense of a free flux and flow between people and had not yet understood how separated by race, class, education, region, religion or politics adults can become. Nor had I any inkling of how complicated it can be for adult couples to make friends.

Patricia had belonged to my father's church before marrying Waylan. When Patricia introduced them to Waylan, he won them over. He was "colorful"; he was "a live wire" and "a lot of fun." They became friends partly because Frank and May, my mother and father, were not strictly a unit. My mother dutifully carted casseroles to potluck suppers and socialized with the congregation, but she never once went to church with my father and me. Being a captive of the Southern Baptists had stuck in her craw; she believed in dancing, she'd take a drink (one only — a second made her laugh too loudly), and she'd smoke a cigarette while having that drink, though without fully inhaling. She had a narrow but distinct streak of iconoclasm that came from growing up on the Brontes, the Romantic poets, and Dickens. My father's congregation were mostly white-collar professionals (the next step up was Episcopal, but that was too close to being Catholic), and so May never had to endure the rant of bigots on the subjects of intoxication and integration, but those Presbyterian ladies and gentlemen were maybe a tad too conventional to interest her. Waylan, on the other hand, drank and smoked too much, listened to kicker music and played poker, but he had none of the vicious, provincial earmarks of the garden-variety redneck. He was funny, loved to dance. He had good manners. He was like a riverboat gambler but not so slick you were suspicous of him. Maybe she had half a crush on him.

Thinking back on it, I suppose it was a cross-gender friendship because my father and Patricia might have also made a pair; they served on the Christian Education Committee together (I associate "stewardship" with them both). She had come west right out of Stevens College to teach junior-high English and had married a local lawyer, who was drafted and sent to Korea, where he died. She was tall, long-legged, and slender, with perky good looks and a decided air of "good breeding." Years later I never watched "The Mary Tyler Moore Show" without recalling her.

I don't know how she met Waylan, but they were married by our minister, and she seemed set on bringing him into the fold. Eavesdropping on my parents, I learned that some thought Waylan was a step down for Patricia. His grammar was poor; he seemed to own no footwear other than boots, and all his shirts had pearl buttons; his livelihood was borderline disreputable, and he often looked and admitted to being hung over.

My parents were happy that Patricia had found such a lively, vigorous man to snap her out of her grief. "She just adores him," said my mother, seeming to praise Patricia for her healthy emotional state. Fortunately, Waylan was cheerful and gregarious, casually ignoring those who snubbed him and charming those who didn't. When the church held its periodic square dance, he took over the role of caller. For these dances, Patricia — dubbed "Patty" on the hand-tooled western belt Waylan had made for her — came dolled up in a white Stetson, tight pants, boots, and a scarf. She made a fetching cowgirl, though I never got used to this Dale Evans costume after seeing her at school in shirtwaist dresses and her hair in a French twist.

If he made her more "western," she worked on him, too. She cringed over Waylan's grammar and the country idioms that were so natural to his speech. She quickly bowdlerized his favorites, so that where once he'd uttered, "Whew! It's raining like a cow pissing on a flat rock!" now he said "cow peeing on a flat rock," a more genteel version but one lacking precision and color. "Busier than a one-legged Chinaman in uh ass-kicking contest" became "busier than a one-legged Chinaman playing hopscotch."

By contrast to Waylan, my father was very much a model gentleman who had never delivered any unpleasant surprises to anyone associated with him. For Patricia that quality must have been a welcome foil to her husband's worrisome unpredictability.

The four of them played bridge, canasta, and poker during the few months they were all friends, they danced and dined at the country club more times than in the previous several years my parents had belonged; they went to square dances and "tacky parties," and twice we all made weekend trips to a lake near Lubbock where Waylan had a house-boat, a legacy from his other life, whatever that had been. He also owned a speedboat and skis and liked to be on the water. In his bathing trunks, he was thick-chested, like Robert Mitchum, and he always made certain the ice chest was full of beer, while my father always checked to see that life belts were present. Patricia — "Mrs. Kneu" to me — wore a red one-piece bathing suit and was much bigger-breasted than I'd known. I could guess why Waylan had willingly married so many social problems and tried so hard to fit into a circle where he must have felt a vulgar intruder. He must have welcomed my parents' friendship with an especially piquant eagerness and appreciation, and so the day he hired me to help deliver the jukebox, he was trying to repay what he took to be my parents' kindness in over-looking his deficiencies of breeding and character.

One day when I came home Waylan was sitting at the kitchen table with my mother. They were drinking coffee. Waylan was smoking a Pall Mall. They looked faintly sheep-ish, a little rattled; Waylan's eyes were red, and my mother rose to begin peeling potatoes the instant I ambled in and greeted them.

"Hello, Sport," said Waylan.

"Take out the trash, will you, dear?" chirped my mother.

I put my books down on the table. I whistled. They said nothing. I cleared my throat, tied my laces, took the trash can from under the sink, opened the lid, stomped on the trash to compact it. I wanted to prevent them from contin-uing whatever they were doing when I had come in. I didn't know what it was, only that they'd obviously been talking about something important, dramatic. If I couldn't stop them, I wanted to hang around to hear more, though I knew nobody would say anything that mattered with me present.

I dashed out to the alley, dumped the trash, and scurried back thinking that I might catch a word or two going in or that what they were up to might leave a scent, figuratively speaking. But I heard a car door slam, an engine start, and Waylan's El Camino pull away from the house.

"What'd he want?" I meant to be casual about his being here, but, to my surprise, I sounded hostile.

"None of your business."

Strangely, this reply soothed me, partly because I heard it often — any time my curiosity overstepped the bounds of propriety. Many aspects of adult life were NOYB: how much money my father made or how much had been spent on any household item or gift, what the suppositories in the refrigerator were used for, and why my cousin had left town for several months after being "jilted" and where, exactly, she'd gone. So the kitchen conversation was simply another item added to the list.

Boy Scouts met Tuesday nights at the church, and as I was pedalling out our driveway on my bike, Patricia Kneu pulled up in a blue Packard I'd never seen before. Getting out, she waved and smiled at me as if we hadn't met in months, though I'd seen her at school that afternoon with a yellow tissue clutched in her fist, and I could recognize a "big brave smile."

My curiosity now became a roaring fire fanned by these two extraordinary but separate visits from Mr. and Mrs. Kneu, but I couldn't learn more without feigning an illness and hanging around to eavesdrop, and that would mean shirking my duty as leader of the Phantom Buffalo Patrol.

It was pointless to ask my parents anything. I watched

Patricia Kneu carefully at school over the next few days. She looked pained, drawn, tired. The Kneus and my parents didn't go out together for a few weeks, though each appeared again at our house separately two other times when I was scheduled to be absent. Once when Patricia came my mother sent me on an unnecessary errand. I got back in time to hear Patricia sobbing in my parents' bedroom, and I stood dumbfounded for a moment in the foyer, listening.

My father was in the living room calmly reading a newspaper.

"Where's Mother?"

"Well," he mused, as if making an educated guess, "I think she's in the bedroom with Mrs. Kneu." I didn't ask what they were doing because the sobs were perfectly audible, and my father had answered as if they were only discussing a dress pattern.

During this time, my parents fell silent when I walked into a room. Neither Waylan nor Patricia Kneu was referred to in casual conversation. Once I thought Patricia Kneu might not be as strict as my parents about what was my business, so at school I said to her, "Would you please tell Mr. Kneu I'd be glad to help him this Saturday if he needs anything done?" I'd hoped that just mentioning her husband would inspire her to spill her guts. She said, "Yes, of course."

On a Wednesday, my mother said, "We're all going to Lake Arrowhead on Sunday. Perhaps you'd like to invite Darrell or Bobby to come."

Storm must've blown over, I thought. I asked Darrell to come because he was always willing to sneak off with a stolen cigarette and talk about girls and guns and whether Ford was better than Chevy. I promised to show him the French tickler, and he said he'd bring his brother's cartoon book from Juarez that showed Blondie and Dagwood doing it.

On Sunday morning, Darrell and I were sitting on my lawn loading our Daisy Red Ryders with BBs when Waylan's El Camino pulled up. In the passenger seat was a woman I'd never seen.

"Say, Sport!" Waylan's bicep was flattened on the window sill, distending his anchor tatoo. "Your folks about ready?"

"I think so."

Waylan got out, then lifted his ice chest from the bed of the El Camino and carried it over to our Chrysler woody. The woman emerged and stood stretching in the sunlight. Darrell and I exchanged a look.

"Marilyn Monroe," Darrell whispered.

She had on tight red shorts and high-heeled sandals and a yellow cotton blouse tied at her midriff, disclosing a flat tan belly. Her blonde hair was piled up and tied with a scarf, and her sunglasses were propped on her forehead. Her huge plastic earclips were replicas of oranges. On one wrist was a man's ID bracelet, and on the other large plastic rings that matched the earclips.

She smiled right at us. "Hi y'all."

"Hi, ma'am." We rose and stood trembling. "My name's James," I offered. "I live here. And this is Darrell."

"My name's Noreen. Y'all got a bathroom?"

I heard steel guitars. "Oh, sure! Come on in!"

Leading her up the flagstone walk, I got too far ahead because she was a little shaky on those heels. I caught a whiff of alcohol on the breeze. Once I stopped, smiling, and waited, an eager, considerate host. When she walked, her bracelets clicked like loud knitting needles. I didn't know why, but even though I was surprised to see her, I was glad she was here.

"Actually," I said as I ushered her into the foyer, "We have two bathrooms."

She grinned and winked. "I just need one that works! That beer just runs right through me, and I need to pee so bad I can taste it!"

I laughed and led her to the bathroom off the guest bedroom, where I stood too long as she danced in place, pointing out the new towels that had been hanging there for years and telling her the medicine chest had stuff if she needed anything.

I went down the hall toward the kitchen. It seemed urgent that I report her presence to my mother. I could picture her in that dove-gray bathroom, her in those bright colors, bracelets rattling, needing to pee so bad she could "taste it." I hoped she didn't say anything like that around my mother, and I wondered suddenly if my parents had been expecting this Noreen.

My mother was packing her wicker picnic basket. The window near her elbow looked onto the street, and I could see Waylan moving about our woody. My father was with him now, and Darrell had been put into service as a bearer. Had she seen Noreen? Wearing penny loafers, blue jeans with a side zipper, a blouse and cardigan sweater, my mother could have been ordered from L.L. Bean, but I thought she looked like a Polish farm wife compared to the stranger in our bathroom.

"Mr. Kneu is here. Noreen's in the bathroom."

"Noreen." It was not a question; she was recording the information.

"Yeah, the woman who came with Mr. Kneu."

"Oh, yes. All right." She closed the lid on the basket and handed it to me.

"Who is she, anyway?"

I expected to hear NOYB, but she said, "Why, I suppose she's a friend of his. He mentioned he might bring one."

Just as my father had been deaf to Patricia's sobbing in his own bedroom, now my mother pretended nothing was strange about Waylan's leaving Patricia at home and bringing this Noreen instead.

Noreen appeared in the kitchen doorway and leaned one hip against the frame.

"Y'all sure got a pretty house!" She smiled at me, then carried the smile like a canape on a tray and served it to my mother. "I just love that blue bedspread and them pictures with the blue frames and that nice double wedding ring quilt on that cedar chest. My granny made quilts like that and she give me a bunch but I lost ever damn one of them because I move around so much, you know, and the trailer I live in's so teeny you can't hardly turn around in it, and it just kills me now to think of her working so hard and me not taking any better care than I did, what with letting this boyfriend I had's dog have puppies on one."

There was a pause. "Thank you," said my mother.

My heart went out to Noreen. My mother's small slice of unconventionality would never stretch so far to cover all the sins Noreen unwittingly confessed in one short speech. I hoped my mother wouldn't embarrass me by shunning her.

"Mother," I said, "this is Noreen. Noreen, this is mother."

"May." Smiling with pained bemusement, my mother extended her hand, which puzzled Noreen for a moment, but then Noreen reached out, bracelets clacking and red nails flashing, and they briefly pincered the ends of each other's fingers.

Noreen followed me out of the house. I put the picnic basket in the wagon while she surveyed the landscape with one haunch pressed against the fender and her sunglasses slid down like a visor over her eyes. Waylan and my father came over from the El Camino, and Waylan said, "Frank, this is Noreen. Noreen, Frank."

My father looked her over much too quickly and crowed, "Well, it's very nice to meet you!"

"Same here," said Noreen. "Any friend of Pooter's."

"Aw, Noreen."

"What!?"

"Nothing," muttered Waylan.

During the ride to Lake Arrowhead, my parents had the front seat, Waylan and Noreen were behind them, and Darrell and I sat in the rear with the life vests, picnic basket, and ice chest. I'd never noticed that Waylan had a bald spot where Jewish boys wore yarmulkes. Sitting just behind Noreen, I smelled beer and her heady floral perfume. Her collar had a faint grime ring, and you could see the dark roots of her hair. The more I knew of her, the more I ached with a sorrowing desire.

"I love these big old station wagons," Noreen said to the adults. "Don't you, Pooter? I wish you'd get one instead of driving that Chevy with that teeny little old cab." She leaned forward and stuck her head over the front seat. "First time he picked me up in it, this friend I have, Emily Dorcus? that works with me at the Longhorn she said that El Camino looks like a pimp-mobile. I told her I'd damn sure take it over what I seen her boyfriend pick her up in — it's one of them Nashes that's got the seat that lays back, you know? because you can't ride in it without people thinking the worst, and I said to her that at least in Pooter's pickup people know there can't be no hanky-panky in bucket seats!" She laughed and slapped the top of the seat. Dust rose in a cloud. "She was just jealous, anyway, idden that right, Pooter?"

"No comment. I'll take the fifth. Or maybe even a quart if you keep it up."

"Well, it's true!" She turned back to the front. "When he come in the first time she's the one pointed him out to me. He sat down at a table in my station and don't you know she tried to jump it? She like to had a hissy fit when I made her back off." Noreen whirled, and, grinning, slapped Waylan on his arm. "I bet you didn't even know that, did you, Pooter?"

"I guess not."

"I guess you didn't see it when she dropped her name and telephone number on a cocktail napkin, either?"

"It was a case of mistaken identity."

"Mistaken identity!" Noreen hooted. "I brought him a refill and saw it sitting there and I just snatched it up like it was trash. I don't think he ever would of ast me out if he wadden trying to get that napkin back!"

"Aw, hell, Noreen. That's not true." Waylan grinned. As she leaned forward, the small of her back was exposed. Waylan casually laid his palm there, his fingers easing under the waistband of the shorts, and caressed her. She turned, winked at him, then they kissed with a smack. She bent forward again, poking her face into the front seat. My father was studiously driving while my mother had an unopened book in her lap. "How did y'all meet?"

I strained forward. I'd never heard word one about my parents' courtship; it was as if they'd been married at birth. Seconds lapsed before my mother, recovering, was able to say, "It was at a dance, a sorority dance."

"Aw, now that's romantic! Pooter, how come you and me couldn't of met that way?"

"Because I didn't belong to no sorority."

I wanted Noreen to ask them how old they were, what they said and wore, but their love life ran a poor second to her favorite subject. We heard how Noreen had growed up in Fort Smith, Arkansas, moved to Big Spring when she was in grammar school, was Queen of the Howard County Rodeo when she was sixteen — still got the clippings and she'll show us some time? — then she left school to work at the air base in Abilene, got married to and divorced from an airman all in one month, went to beauty school but couldn't stand the stink. Now she lives in a trailer park with a cocker spaniel named Bobo and cat named Mitsy, loves Coors but hates Pabst because it tastes just like alligator piss, and can't stand Mexican food because it looks like something the dog already ate. She loves Carl Perkins and listens to "The Louisiana Hayride" from Shreveport, and the best thing about Waylan is the cute way he looks just like a little boy when he first gets up in the mornings with his hair sticking up all over.

My mother said, "Umm!" or "My goodness!" or "That's nice!" while her fingers riffled pages of her book.

I couldn't get enough of Noreen, even though in one hour I had learned more about her and about Waylan than I had in all the months of knowing the Kneus. I could picture where and how she lived and, as I watched Waylan's hand linger on her waist, I could even imagine them lying on a bed and kissing like people in the movies.

However, my liking Noreen and being aroused by her seemed vaguely disloyal, and I did worry about Mrs. Kneu. Wasn't my parents' toleration a betrayal, too? Did Mrs. Kneu know we were here with Noreen? I pictured Mrs. Kneu at home alone crying, a tissue wadded in her fist. I could vividly recall her sobs coming from my parents' bedroom and my own astonishment on hearing a grown woman, a teacher, cry from a broken heart.

Waylan's houseboat looked like a trailerhouse on pontoons at its dockside mooring. We arrived about noon; Waylan, my father, and Darrell went to gas up the outboard and to ready our gear for skiing while my mother set out lunch on the table. Noreen wanted to help; my mother let her remove the lids from the Tupperware containers and locate serving spoons.

"Oh, this looks so good! I just love deviled eggs. I have to tell you I'm real put out with Waylan for not letting me know we was going to be picnicking, or I would of brought something for sure, May."

"Oh, don't let it worry you. I brought plenty. I know Waylan."

I don't know what Noreen presumed we'd be eating, but my mother had packed both her own share and things Patricia would've brought.

"Have y'all known him long?"

Noreen shot me a quick sideways glance; she wanted my mother to herself. But I was not going to budge until ordered away.

"Since about this time last year."

Noreen bit off the end of a carrot stick with a pop.

"I guess y'all know his ex-wife."

"His ex-wife?"

"Patricia."

My mother was scooping tuna salad out of a bowl onto a plate of lettuce leaves; after a moment's hesitation not quite hidden by her task, she said, "Yes, we've known Patricia for a pretty good while." She turned to the sink and ran water into the bowl. "Are you certain she's an ex?"

"Well, maybe not yet. But she will be if it's up to me." Noreen tried to toss this off lightly with a laugh, but failed.

My mother ducked her head to open the compartment under the sink. "I'm sure that's true." Though muffled, her voice had an icy edge.

Noreen didn't hear it. "That bitch is not going to get the best of me, I can tell you that right now."

My mother looked pointedly at me. "Go tell the men that lunch is ready."

On the way to the service pier, I realized that the Kneus were about to get divorced. That seemed terrible. I'd never known anyone divorced. I associated it with honky-tonk songs about cheatin', leavin', drinkin', lyin', and cryin', so I could see how it could happen to Waylan, but not to Mrs. Kneu. It wouldn't happen to my parents, either. Or to me.

I don't know what my mother said to Noreen about the Kneus, but when we men returned from the service pier, Noreen was leaning against the rail outside and smoking. Inside, my mother told us, "The table's not big enough for us all. Just take a plate and we'll buffet it."

Darrell and I took our plates onto the deck. The wind was blowing grit and a bank of grey cloud had slid beneath the sun. Between bites of cold fried chicken and potato salad, we plinked with our BB guns at cans and bottles we tossed into the water. In almost every war movie, a soldier or a sailor got a Dear John letter. A scene like that usually came before a big battle, and more often than not, getting a Dear John marked a man for certain death.

"You think Louise Bowen is good-looking?" I asked.

"Yeah, she's ok."

"I might ask her to go steady."

"Have you got to first base with her?"

"Oh, yeah. Sure."

"Second base?"

I'd never analyzed the analogy closely. First base must mean kissing Louise on the mouth; second was also above her waist, but I had no idea how you knew you'd "gotten" to third and home plate. On the hay ride I'd been too devoted to trying to feel her right breast to imagine anything else.

"Yeah."

Darrell opened his cannister of BBs, sipped from it, then picked BBs off his lips one by one and loaded them into the magazine.

"Did do det to turd bayth?"

"No. Her mother was home."

Darrell spied a lizard onshore and went off to stalk it, and I carried our plates into the kitchen. My parents were sitting at the table drinking coffee with an air of serenity, as if silence were sunshine and they were basking in it.

"Where's Mr. Kneu and Noreen?"

"They're changing," said my mother.

I set the plates in the sink. From behind the bedroom door, we heard Noreen wail, "It is not, Waylan!" A low masculine murmur, then another protest from Noreen. My father was smiling around the stem of his pipe. My mother, looking at him, raised her eyebrows.

"What was that — " I aped her raised eyebrows — "For?"

"None of your business!" declared my father.

A squeak from the bedroom door, then rustling as Noreen and Waylan stepped down the tiny hallway. Meanwhile, Darrell appeared in the galley door, holding a bleeding lizard by its tail. When Noreen came into view I heard a collective gasp.

"Y'all don't think this looks tacky, do you?"

This appeal was pointed at me, but I couldn't look at her directly. I wasn't old enough. She was wearing the first bikini I had ever encountered personally, though I'd seen pictures of French women wearing them in Life. Noreen's was polka-dotted. Darrell was blushing. My father dug his multi-faceted tool from his pocket and used it to run maintenance on his pipe. I chanced looking at Noreen above the neck. Her eyes were red, and her chin was quivering. Waylan stood over her shoulder hang-dog, rolling his eyes.

"I didn't say it was tacky, Noreen, I said — "

She whirled on Waylan. "No, but that's what you were thinking!"

I now had my first dorsal view. Darrell and I grinned at each another.

She turned to my mother. "He just dudden know fashion! It has a little jacket I was going to wear except in the water!"

"I'm sure it would have been fine," murmured my mother.

Noreen accosted Waylan, pecking at the air with her head. "See!"

She stormed back toward the bedroom. Waylan gave us a sheepish, doleful grin, then followed her.

My mother sat fully clothed in a lawn chair on the deck reading her book. My father, Darrell, and I ran the outboard awhile and skiied. On one pass, Waylan hailed us from the pier. He had two six-packs under his arm, and during the next hour or so, he drank eight beers. My father had one and drove the boat while Waylan played out the rope for us. He didn't ski. He tried to be in good humor, but as time went on the alcohol got the best of him, and when he wasn't aware of being watched his eyes darkened and his lips had a sour-lemon twist.

The weather turned blustery; gusting winds and sand turned the water choppy, and the sky had a white cloud glaze that diluted the sunshine. We called it quits. My father and Darrell went to the houseboat to rouse the women and to snack, and I stayed with Waylan to pack up the boating gear. I coiled the long yellow ski-rope on my arm the way I'd seen electricians do their cords and thought of how I could ask Waylan about his wife.

As Waylan was folding the life preservers and stowing them in the bow, I said, "Mr. Kneu, your friend Noreen is a real nice lady." I never could have added *In spite of what my mother thinks* but I tried to imply it.

"Aw, God!" groaned Waylan. "She's just a lounge lizard, son. It'd take fifteen of her to equal one good woman."

He opened a beer and sat on the gunwhale. He looked

off over the water and clucked his tongue. Tears welled in his eyes, and he stood at once and busied himself with unhooking the fuel line from the tank to the engine. "Let me tell you something. You get a good one, you stay with her. You start looking around, you find one like your mother or Patricia, you hear?"

"Sir?"

He straightened and looked at me. He wiped his eyes on his bare bicep and snuffled. I was awe-struck. I had never seen a man cry, not even my father. "I guess you know about us splitting the blanket."

"Splitting the blanket?"

He smiled, amused. "Divorce, son. Haven't you ever heard of that?"

I nodded. But I didn't know what it called for, what sort of future it implied, and I was intensely curious about his divorce. I was frightened to see him upset, but so long as he was willing to talk, I had to take advantage of the moment.

I took a breath, counted to ten, then made myself ask, "Sir, how come you and Mrs. Kneu are getting a divorce?"

"How come?" He looked into the sky and squinted, hands on his hips. Then he shrugged. "I don't know." (I didn't believe that then, but I do now.)

He went back to coiling the black fuel line around itself. After a moment, he stopped, looked at me and grinned. "You use that rubber yet?"

"No, Sir."

"Good."

Waylan never double-dated with my parents again or even came to our home. We saw Patricia Kneu at church socials, but she visited us only with groups. I was relieved — maybe divorce was like a poisonous gas. Now and then

I'd see Waylan in the El Camino, a jukebox or pinball machine strapped onto its back; he'd wave, I'd wave back. I dreaded these unexpected encounters because I was afraid he'd ask me about the condom.

I was half-ashamed of not having used it, even if Waylan found it commendable. Having it in my wallet was like having been given a new bicycle only to have it stored in the garage because there was no safe place to ride it. I wanted to "try it out on" Louise, as if it were a tool. I had many questions, but the condom had come without an instruction manual. Were you supposed to put Vaseline on it? Did you put it on before you left the house? Would Louise know what it was? I hoped not; I wanted to think she was virginal, yet I also hoped she knew enough that I wouldn't have to utter any embarrassing explanations. She was a member of my Presbyterian youth group; her parents knew my own. She made good grades. Once she said, apropos of nothing, "Boys are so nasty!" Nothing about her suggested she might recognize a condom, and the more I thought of "using it on her," the more it seemed like a very vulgar joke — fake puke, a fart cushion, or, worse yet, an ugly prank that might go bad and hurt somebody.

One afternoon in a fit of self-loathing over my cowardice, I finished my paper route in lightning speed and tore down to the drug store, where I bought a vial of Prince Matchiabelli's "Wind Song" — that little crownshaped bottle was winningly clever — then I pedalled over to Louise's.

While her mother was cooking dinner, Louise was listening to "This Old House" over and over on her record player, doing her algebra homework, and keeping her four-year-old sister out of her mother's hair. She was supposed to be practicing the piano, she said. Her room was strewn with Golden Books and dolls, and on her bedside table was a pink plate with one last chocolate-chip cookie I didn't have the nerve to ask for. She was still wearing her school clothes — a calf-length plaid skirt and a white cotton blouse.

"What's this for?" she asked as I handed her the perfume.

"Just because."

She nodded toward her dresser. "I got some already."

I shrugged. "Do you remember the hay ride?"

"Yeah, sure." She blushed.

"Lu-lu, come play with me!" her sister demanded. She'd erected a tent by tossing the bedspread over two chairs and had made a nest under it with pillows and dolls.

"In a minute!" Louise snapped.

"I sure had fun," I said.

"Yeah. The bonfire was really neat. I really like 'Smores, too."

Her mother yelled from the kitchen, "Louise, I want you to set the table."

"All right!" Louise hollered back. "In a minute."

I didn't know that this wasn't a good time: I had no notion of the importance of timing in human affairs. I was disappointed that for Louise the high point of the hay ride had been the menu. Maybe she didn't even know she'd been felt up.

"I have to set the table."

I presumed for a moment I could wait for her, but the way she poised expectantly on the bed looking up at me, I could tell she meant the interview had ended. The condom in my wallet crossed my mind for the first time since I'd gotten there, but I hadn't the faintest hope of bringing it up, or even much interest. Louise's sister, the busy household, and, above all, the way every iota of my attention was magnetized by all the complex delicacy of Louise's ears, her eyelashes, cheekbones, her mouth and neck — there was no space left for anything as foreign to us both as this device in my hip pocket.

"I just thought maybe you didn't have any perfume." I was trying to find a graceful exit. "A woman on my route gave it to me. I could let my mother have it if you don't like it."

"Oh, no, I like it. I have some, I said." She lifted the bottle to the light and reappraised it. I think she'd just realized that a boy had brought her a gift. She unscrewed the little black cap and inhaled.

"This smells better than what I got." She smiled fetchingly and held it up for me to sniff. Standing over her, I put my hand about hers to steady the bottle. Smelling the perfume while looking at her hazel eyes and the tendrils of blonde hair falling over her forehead and her freckled cheeks made me swoon. Her blouse buttoned down the front, and the lapels framed her flushed and freckled neck, her chest, and the swellings that vanished under her brassiere.

She leaned forward, allowing me a better look. Seeing the slim white edge of that undergarment made me sick with desire. I thought I'd buy a "broken heart" charm; her half would hang from a gold chain around her neck and rest in that warm, freckled place between her breasts.

The condom was still in my wallet when school ended and Louise went with her family to Maine. In my weekly vigils in the Civil Defense tower, I mooned about her while scanning the skies. I was a wounded G.I. who hobbled on a crutch; a nurse, she walked beside me with my arm over her shoulder for support. High school boys yelled ugly things at her from cars; I yanked open their doors and dragged them out to give them tremendous thrashings. I had my own car, and she was with me, wearing that white cotton blouse. This smells better than what I got. Her smile, my hand on hers, those hazel eyes, her flushed neck, the achingly sweet swellings under that crescent of brassiere — as I remembered, my hands left damp imprints on the binoculars. Our future was a pot over which I watched with enormous impatience, and I desperately flung myself ahead to August 21st, the day her letter said she was coming back. I peered anxiously into the horizon for whatever enigmatic fulfillment was winging toward me. For years I thought that because nothing ever happened I had nothing to remember.

The
Plantation
Club

William "Stoogie" Clark stepped off the bus in our town with an alto sax and a suitcase of uniform remnants from a band that collapsed in El Paso. Like our Chicano migrants-turned-residents and redneck roustabouts, he'd stopped to recoup the means to move on and never made it. Mornings he washed dishes at the Winslow Cafe. Three nights a week he played at The Plantation, a nightclub in our small black ghetto.

Windowless but for the portholes head-high along the front, the club had the air of a sternwheeler in dry-dock. A plantation scene embellished the expanse of stucco above the portholes — a cotton patch with an Aunt Jemima, a veranda where a colonel with a cigar chatted with a brace of belles. The street in front of the club was washboard sand littered with shards of glass; here black whores meandered along the shoulders. We junior classmen cruised this block with only a driver visible and three or four others huddled on the floorboards.

"Hey, wheah you goin', boy?"

"Lookin' for some poontang."

"You lookin' right at it!"

"How much?"

"They's different kinds!"

"Well, I like it hot and greasy, Mama!"

"Lawd! You don't look that rich!"

Then we'd all spring upright, cackle *yah yah yah*, and leave a wash of sand spray to flap her skirt as we sped away, victors again, but over what we never knew. We didn't harass them as much after they started calling us "Cig - uh - RET Pee -tuhs."

Maybe that's why we didn't hear Stoogie until the summer before our senior year when Terry and I decided a little banter could liven up the night. With two of us the game was limited to an exchange that stalemated when we had to put up or shut up, but it beat going into orbit around the Sonic Dog, and we had already spent an hour on the main drag looking for that mythical nymphomaniac we dreamed would pull up in her Caddy convertible and bare her breasts.

Drifting slowly by The Plantation, we heard an alto rise into melancholy flight on the opening bars of "'Round Midnight." Confused, I thought I was hearing a record, but even that would have been a marvel: my gods — Bird, John Coltrane, Sonny Stitt, Sonny Rollins, Stan Getz, Cannonball Adderly — were so obscure in my town that to ask for an album by one at the music store was like asking for the latest from The Outer Mongolian Preschool Rhythm Band and Chorus in Concert. We had stumbled onto jazz via "Moonglow with Martin" on WWL in New

Orleans, and we had spent countless nights since riding in our parents' cars listening to music such as we had never dreamed existed broadcast from twelve hundred miles away by crow-fly and a century or so by cultural disposition to our remote corner of New Mexico. Barely a decade out of its boom, our overgrown crossroad had a ragged, honky-tonk energy, but it was cowboy country, and we felt misplaced in it, practitioners of an alien religion.

Terry stopped the car. We heard the opening phrase repeated with a minor variation in the fifth bar, the sound not exactly angry but anguished: midnight was a dark sponge soaking up every man's hope and illusion. Maybe that's too heavy, but we were stunned.

We parked across the street and listened to that alto do its tricks on "C-Jam Blues," "How High The Moon," "A-Train," "Bye Bye Blackbird," and three more blues, each in a different key. Now and then a black face poked its way into our windows, but we made no requests and sat for an hour, astonished that such a sound existed so far from either coast.

After a lull, four men came out a side door. Guessing they were the group, we decided to brave asking if we could listen inside. As we walked toward the club, we got nervous. Our town was relatively peaceful; our schools had integrated soon after the Brown decision without much flap save a plethora of hysterical sermons delivered on the eve of the Apocalypse by our good Baptist brethren. But this wasn't our turf. The uncharted territory around the building hid conspirators whose razors flashed at the corners of my eyes. But wasn't I safe? Hadn't I once shocked my Tennessee relatives by shaking hands with a waiter at their country club? Justice always saw that the pure-hearted were protected and that bigots got their due.

We came up to the men at the door. In the dimness they

were only vague shapes, but soon features emerged which
I'd come to know well over the next year: R.B., the huge,
affable drummer who worked days loading blocks of ice
onto waiting trucks and who had been a Golden Gloves
champ; Candy, the piano man, a small Mescalero-Apache
with a cataract on his left eye; Scratchmo, the eldest, with a
thicket of wiry gray hair around his face — he spat tobacco
juice into a coffee can perched atop the amplifier of his guitar; he always wore a red woolen shirt (hence his name)
under faded denim overalls, and displayed a perpetual half-
smirk so ambivalent that even a year later I hadn't learned
to decipher it. And, finally, there was Stoogie, a caramel-
colored man whose baggy eyelids drooped as though he
was forever on the verge of sleep — and who now lounged
against the building with one sole flat against the wall, his
cigarette an orange arc as he raised it to his lips.

"Hey, you guys are really good!" declared Terry. "We've
been out in the car digging your jazz!"

Scratchmo spat a gob of Beechnut juice onto the sand.
"Hear that, Stoogie? These boys been digging our jazz."

Stoogie didn't straighten from his slump; only a flicker of
his drooping eyelids suggested he was conscious of us.

"It's in the air," he muttered. He pushed away from the
wall and headed back inside the building, followed by
Candy and Scratchmo. R.B. hung back.

"Y'all not old enough to drink, are you?"

"No sir," I mumbled.

"Haw!" He ducked his head toward the door and
winked. "Anybody ask, you say you're with R.B., hear?"

Grateful, we scurried in behind him. The interior of the
club smelled of beer and stale smoke; the crowd filled the
intermission lull with loud talk and laughter. Trying not to
lollygag, we aped the pose of jaded nightlife connoisseurs as
we threaded our way through the occupied tables. Sitting

just in front of the bandstand we watched Stoogie ease down into a metal folding chair and pull his alto out of its open case. It was silver; I knew it had to be a Strad of saxes — a jazz counterpart of Jascha Heifetz would need a "fine" instrument — but soon I found out it was a crappy axe, one of the worst. The soft metal keys were always bending, which kept the pads from seating properly, and it was so out of tune with itself that Stoogie had to adjust each note with his ear and embouchure as he played. It was his tenth horn in as many years — he was broke so often that hocking them was his only resort, though his Otto Link mouthpiece had been carried from one to the next.

Sagging in his chair like a sack of grain, Stoogie descended into "Summertime." A reedy edge serrated the contours of his voice, and he cut into the melody as if easing a knife into the jugular of a drowsy hog. The "high cotton" and "easy livin'" in the lyrics would seem to call for waltz-time on a banjo, but the melody contains more than a whiff of danger and despair, and Stoogie's first chorus ripped that disparity completely apart — his "summertime" was a stoop where junkies nodded, an alley where dark promises were kept.

Mouth agape, I gawked while phrases blossomed from the bell of the horn. We sat five feet away, feeling faint huffs of breath from the horn, the strain of melody and improvised line as tangible as a string of sausages in the air before us. He began to sweat and his cheeks bellowed as he finished his fourth chorus and began working seriously to sign his name across the face of the tune. The dancers were warming up, too, waving and yelling as if his solo were the last lap turn in an evangelical sermon. Had I looked around, I might have recognized them as the minor actors in the dramas played out by the oil-rich whites in town — janitors, maids, junkmen, yard boys, shine boys, dishwashers, and short-order cooks — but I was too dazed to notice.

When Stoogie was through, Scratchmo broke into laughter. "That's all right, man! All *right*!"

Stoogie acknowledged the claps and whistles with a nod but gave no sign he was pleased with himself.

"Man, I gotta get on the elevator," he said to Scratchmo. He got up slowly, trudged off the stand and out the side door. The trio went into "Rock Me Baby, All Night Long," with Scratchmo doing a passable imitation of Big Joe Williams.

After the gig, the quartet went separate ways, but before the club closed we bought R.B. a beer and pumped him for information. Stoogie had grown up on Chicago's South Side, dropped out of the eighth grade to make a flight from the ghetto with an r-and-b band, married at eighteen, lost his wife to a pimp and gave up their child for adoption, took up with another woman who OD'd on heroin, spent a hitch in the Navy, then drifted along the California coast playing in clubs and working menial day-jobs. He hit the bigtime briefly as a sideman with Billy Eckstine's band, but in New York he was swamped by squalor and bad luck — busted, he served a two-year sentence for possession of marijuana. Man! I thought. Stoogie's really paid some dues! Terry and I were unscathed by divorce, disfigurement, or poverty; our mothers made sure we got fresh vegetables and clean underwear, and our fathers had taught us how to shake hands and use hammers, pull triggers and paddle canoes. Our greatest living enemy was neither want nor oppression but the rampant rashes of acne which we tried to banish with soaps and creams and a half-hour spent harvesting the night's crop at the mirror before dashing off to school feeling like exhibitions of running sores. My greatest sorrow to date was having lost my first love to another at age fifteen.

Sooner or later I'd be in luck and a tragedy would really

scar me. In the meantime, I'd have to settle for working on technique. We showed up at the Plantation every weekend night, and after a while, we talked the group into letting us bring our horns. We would scrunch down against the back wall and try to hit the vein with the needle as the quartet roared away, creating a very soft but discordant clarinet and trumpet duet under them which must have sounded like an untuned radio to anyone out front. Now and then Stoogie'd lean back in his chair and say, "Go watch Candy's hand," and we'd tiptoe across to peer over Candy's shoulder as his left hand graphed out the changes to the tune. Or he'd say, "Harmony!" telling us to play a series of whole notes with the changes.

But I hated clarinet and I'd resolved six months before meeting Stoogie that I had to have a sax, the axe my heroes played. My parents had agreed to provide a matching grant, and I had saved my wages from working after school and on Saturdays delivering pianos. The horn had been on order for a month after I had started going to the club, and I had driven the owner of the store nuts asking about it daily.

When it came, my alto was a brilliant gold hookah asleep in a red velvet pouf. A gen-yew-ine Selmer Mark VI, axe of the gods — *Downbeat* said so. With it I'd wail my way into Birdland with Kenton or Maynard or Art Blakey; I'd be on Ed Sullivan wailing away with my own big band and the girl who'd left me would eat her heart out! Move over, Sonny Rollins! Bite the dust, John Coltrane! A new star had risen!

When I fingered the keys, a soft *poomp* said they seated perfectly on their holes, the pristine leather pads the color of sand. The horn smelled of polish and oil and cork grease, and I gave it a good going over with beady eyes not so much to inspect it but to lay claim to it. I found a deep scratch in the lacquer under the low C key which wouldn't disappear when I rubbed it, so I decided to ignore it.

I was dying to show it off. But driving alone to the club (Terry had the flu), I felt uneasy. The worst player in town had a Selmer Mark VI, the best had a Brand X nickel-plated monster. I kept assuring myself that I had worked like hell to scrape up half the cost and tried to forget that my parents had paid the other half.

Looking it over, Stoogie didn't seem to begrudge my owning it. I invited him to try it out; he slipped his mouthpiece onto it, and when he blew a few scales, I heard the Stoogie-sound with a new perimeter — rounder, more solid, its circumference laced with a fretwork of brass.

"Wow!" He shook his head. "Been a long time, man!" He blew a few more licks, pleased at how his phrases took to the air without much drag. "It's sure easy. This is a nice axe."

"Go ahead and play it," I offered quickly when he started to hand it back.

When the first set began, his solos contained new dimensions, but I was too lost in my skull to study them. He was playing great music on *my* horn, and that gave me hope, as if his improvised lines would stick to the lining of the horn to be unpeeled by my breath. After Stoogie had sort of primed the horn like a handpump on a waterwell, I'd just stick it in my mouth, take a breath, and out would zoom phrases as rich, juicy and evocative as Stoogie's. (No matter that in my room I had gotten nothing but squawks, though the fingering was similar to my clarinet's.) I got itchy to try it out.

But Stoogie wasn't in a hurry to turn it over. One tune led to another; a half-hour went by, then an hour — Stoogie's enjoyment spread to the others, and they began playing into break-time with no desire at all to quit.

What if he couldn't stop playing it? Refused to? On the dance floor, Friday night's drunks were whooping and hollering, and I looked long enough to notice that I was the only white cat here. Although a veil was actually descending over the scene, I could have sworn that one was lifting, one composed of my delusion that we were all bosom buddies of the blue note. When they finished the set and I asked for the horn, Stoogie would give me a droopy-eyed look and say, *Huh? You shoah talkin' some trash, white boy!* I'd treat it as a joke and say, Aw shit, Stoogie! Come on, man, lemme try it! *Hey, Scratchmo! Who's this ofay callin' me Stoogie and jivin' about my axe, huh?* And Scratchmo would guffaw, slap his knee, then turn his sinister gaze to within an inch of my face and say, *Hey, boy! You'd best scat before I cut you three ways — wide, deep, and quite frequently!!* God! How could I prove the horn was mine? That scratch under the C key?

Miserable, I missed what was probably Stoogie's finest work in years, to judge by how everyone carried on when they broke after the set.

"Whew! That's a fine, fine, horn," Stoogie said when he handed it to me. "You better learn how to blow it."

Humbled, I accepted the proverbial boot from teacher to student with a nod. But when I took the horn and slipped the hook of the neckstrap through the holding hole, the horn hung from my neck like a gaudy brass albatross, so heavy I could hardly stand.

I begged off and slunk away. Driving home, I could feel my ears burning. How could I ever do justice to this horn that lay on the back seat of my parents' Ford like hot loot from a burglary? Only by practice could I earn the right to play it. And in return for those unofficial lessons I had taken for granted from Stoogie, I'd. . . save him. It wasn't fair that this black Paganini had to wash dishes at the

Winslow Cafe. I'd talk the city fathers into making him an Honorary Mayor or an Artist in Residence! I'd find him a good gig where nobody would be allowed to request "San Antonio Rose" or "Anniversary Waltz." I'd get all the young musicians in town to chip in to buy him a Mark VI; I'd find a way to get the group on record.

Every morning thereafter my horn reached my mouth when my feet hit the floor. I bought a mouthpiece like Stoogie's. I got to school early to have a half-hour warmup before band, then I'd sneak away from study hall to the bandroom and remain there during lunch hour. I took the horn to work after school so that between deliveries I could play in the stockroom. After work, I'd play before supper and to bedtime, until, with a pair of chops hanging on my mouth like the limp fingers of rubber gloves, I'd put the horn up for the day.

At last I got to solo. A Saturday night and, as they used to say, the joint was jumping. The band had condescended to do "The Hucklebuck," and the air was charged with lascivious electricity as people bucked their huckles. R.B. started hammering out a stripper's beat with cymbal and bass drum crashes on 2 and 4; Stoogie, just returned from taking the elevator, was grinning so hard he could only play greasy honks. He looked back at us and jerked his head toward the mike: Get on up here, one of you!

Heart thudding, my hands suddenly slick, I stumbled toward the mike while the quartet vamped changes. My brain whirled to map out my melodic strategy, trying to recall the notes in those three simple chords, plotting my solo as if I were building a gun rack from a plan in *Popular Mechanics*. I reached the mike, stuck the mouthpiece between my quivering jaws, blew an A in the upper register and held it. Somebody on the dance floor yelled, "Yeah!" Though I'm sure now it was in reply to something

like "Ain't he awful?" which, mercifully, I hadn't heard, I
dreamed that my A was really turning them on; I thanked
my lucky stars for finding it and hung onto it, pausing only
for breath. Along about bar eleven, I saw that I couldn't
get away with taking another chorus with that A — it was
weird, if not monotonous, and Scratchmo would jibe me all
night long about my two-chorus whole note. Something
stunning in contrast was called for, a Yin to the first chorus's Yang, and the solution came in a flash — if I played
enough notes, I was bound to get some right ones in; people would hear those and pick out their own melodic line
from the heap of assorted phrases I would toss onto the air
like articles on a clearance table in a bargain basement. And
if I played fast enough, the clinkers would pass undetected.

It's a blessing no one taped that second chorus; I believe
I played through the entire Universal-Prescott book in
those twelve bars. I left enough "melodies" tangled in the
air that an academy of musicologists could have devoted a
lifetime to unballing them and still could not have seen
through the skein of noise above the bandstand. But I had
lost my musical cherry; I could survive that stretch of
sound-time, and though I was terrible, I knew I couldn't
get worse.

We had come to know the players in a western swing
band at a local honky tonk and found that they too were
jazz buffs, though their axes wouldn't have suggested it.
Gradually I was getting a picture — musicians were poor
outcasts given to fits of insanity; they had vices ranging
from perversions to narcotics to alcohol; they were — in a
word — outlaws. We tried to develop the Outlaw Outlook
as a means of shedding our old skins. We imagined that
The Plantation was our club and that we were inconspicu-
ous there, though how we dreamed two white children in
sunglasses and berets could have gone unnoticed among

two hundred black patrons is a testament to our innocence. At school, Terry and I went about laden with props — cigarette holders a la Dizzy Gillespie, *Downbeat* tucked under our arms. We jived along in a slouch, eyelids drooping, talking hiptalk, feeling more and more alienated from our classmates' concerns for ball games and proms. We gave each other skin, we snapped our fingers and sang complicated scat riffs in those syllables the uninitiated find so strange. We quickly became insufferable, and that only ossified our belief that we were cool. I took to calling everyone, even my mother, "man."

Part of the myth of Jazz Star required that we be out of our skulls as much as possible, so during the spring months we drank a good deal more than we really wanted to. We downed innumerable cases of beer and fifths of bourbon before settling down to the wine of the people, Thunderbird.

Inevitably, we got more curious about Stoogie's dope. We saw it as a must for every Jazz Star's prop locker. Besides washing dishes and playing at the Plantation to keep his household — a Chicana and her four children — together, Stoogie also watered greens at the golf course on weeknights. He was growing his own stuff in a nearby pasture and was looking forward to a bountiful harvest come the fall. He worked out of a shed on the grounds, and sometimes we'd go out there, perch on fertilizer sacks, and listen to "Moonglow" on a portable radio, while he made his rounds changing sprinklers. Stoogie had never offered us any of his homegrown. But neither had he forbidden it, so once when he was out on the course we smoked a joint. When he found us collapsed on the floor, giggling, he said, "You just best be sure when you walkin' on clouds you don't trip over the Man." Point made — we sobered some and ended up at the Sonic Dog ordering triple-decker banana splits, tripping on the lights, and smothering the sillies with sleeves pressed against our mouths. Just your ordinary goofy high school high.

We began taking the elevator with Stoogie at the club, and though it didn't help our playing one iota, doing it enhanced our self-esteem. By August, as we got ready to attend the Berkeley School of Music, we had become unspeakably With It. One night Terry and I got stoned at his crib while we were digging some sides, and when I had to split, the mirror showed me two swollen orbs with a reddish wash against a yellow background. I'd walked over there and I'd have to walk home. Very cleverly, I decided to carry an empty beer can. As I floated home, I smirked — six months prior to this I would've been peeing my pants to think that the Man would catch me with illegal booze, and now here I was — practically a junkie no less — using it as a decoy.

The crash came one night later. Caught smoking by two white patrolmen outside the club after the gig, Stoogie and I and Terry were whisked to the station and separated for questioning before we could gather our wits.

"That colored boy sell you those two sticks of marijuana?"

"No sir!"

"How'd they come to be in your shirt pocket?"

"Nobody sold them to me, I swear!"

Sgt. Johnson was seated behind the chief's desk. He peeled the wrapper from a Snicker's and bit into it.

"Thadwudden whuusss."

"Sir?"

He crushed the wrapper into a ball and pleased himself by scoring in the trash can.

"That wasn't what I asked."

Though Sgt. Johnson had proved himself to be a boor

over the previous twenty minutes, he knew a nonanswer when he heard one. But the primary rule of antiaircraft gunnery is to keep throwing flak until you hit.

"Well, sir, we'd never tried any and we were just curious about it, you know, so we only smoked a little bit and decided we didn't want any more of it, and I really didn't like it much to tell the truth, and I don't think I'd ever do it again." As I squirmed in the hard wooden chair, the beret wadded in my hip pocket pressed into my left ham. The instant we had been arrested, I had slipped my sunglasses into my shirt pocket; I had lost my cigarette holder in the patrol car, and, props gone, I could feel an older self rising to the surface — the youth whose classmates had elected him City Manager for a Day; the Boy Scout of some distinction; the son of decent, tax-paying citizens and church members; the best civics student Miss Hall ever had. I kept blinking — man, this couldn't be happening! We had meant harm to no one, our destinies as Jazz Stars had already been mapped out and the supplies laid by! It would be grossly unjust to have all that interrupted for such a stupid reason as having two joints in my shirt pocket.

But Sgt. Johnson's glare was very real, and I had visions of my brilliant career cut short, my parents disgraced, my teachers despairing, and my unfaithful girl friend secretly exultant that she'd escaped being tied down to a convict.

"Something wrong with your hearing, son?"

"No, sir."

"Then where'd you get the stuff?"

"Found it."

"Aw-huh." He nodded. "Where?"

"Uh. . . it was on the parking lot, you know, out at the Sonic Dog."

"Were you by yourself?"

Haw! I thought. No witnesses, no contradictions.

"Yes, sir."

He smiled. "Maybe they had little tags on them that said, 'Smoke Me, I'm a marijuana cigarette'?"

Did that require an answer? "No, sir."

"Then how'd you know what they were?"

"They just looked. . . funny, you know. Not like regular cigarettes. And they smelled like mari. . . smelled weird, you know? So we just guessed."

"We?"

I flushed. "I mean after I'd already showed it to them."

"Uh-huh. And I reckon you gave some to that colored boy because he wanted to try a little, too."

I nodded.

Sgt. Johnson sighed, rose and paced about the room, then eased a haunch onto the desk. He gave me a benign and fatherly look. "Now, I can tell you aren't a dope addict. I can see how a couple kids out for a lark decide out of curiosity to try the stuff, you see? Maybe you didn't know you can get hooked and start craving it."

I wagged my head to encourage this line of thought. Innocence was my best guise and my spotless record the evidence to give it credibility. He had already asked my name and address and whether I had been in trouble before, to which I had given truthful answers, and it looked as if the end might be in sight. Apparently Sgt. Johnson was going to let me off with a lecture about the evil drug and a warning, and I prepared to tune him out. The chief appeared annually in an all-school assembly to peddle the same propaganda, though with what I'd have to admit was a dramatic flair: he'd hold a heap of grass in his palm and say, "I want anybody who wants some of this to come right down here and I'll give it to them for nothing." Then he'd pull his pistol from his holster. "But he might as well take *this* too because he'll be needing something to put him out of his misery!"

"So you smoked a little marijuana — is that any reason to spend a lot of your young life in jail?" Sgt. Johnson was saying. "I know you don't think so. We ain't out to wreck any lives here. Boys will by boys, we know that."

My head was bobbing madly in agreement: Yessir, two tadpoles curious as coons, that's us, sir, no kidding!

"And you say you found it?"

"Yessir."

"At the Sonic Dog."

I nodded.

"Then why's that other boy say you got it in Juarez?"

Had Terry said that? What did Stoogie say? The accused's right to one phone call popped to mind, but not only would my parents learn where I was, it was a definite sign of noncooperation, and I still hoped I'd be able to talk my way out of the station.

"Well, I didn't. He was just guessing."

"He said y'all both got it there."

All I could do was shrug to suggest that life was full of peculiar circumstances that defied credulity.

He eased his haunch off the desk. "Son, you're starting to piss me off!" He pulled a a key chain from his pocket and jangled the keys as he moved behind the desk. They made a steady *chink* like a stack of coins passed through the fingers. Were those keys to the cells? I shivered. He wasn't buying my story.

"You come in here and start talking like a straight shooter, then you bullshit me when I'm trying my best to appreciate your situation — you think I'm dumb?"

"No, sir."

"I don't have to give you the benefit of the doubt. I can lock you up and charge you with possession right now. You understand? For all I know, you been peddling the stuff — maybe you gave it to them, maybe you sold it!"

"Oh no, sir!"

"I don't have any use at all for a slimy creep that'd get other people hooked just to line his pockets. We can put you away for twenty years for dealing in it — you want that?"

"I swear I wasn't doing that!"

"How about finding it — you swear to that, too?"

I hesitated. "Yes," I said, with less conviction.

He threw up his hands in exasperation. "Well, if you don't beat all!" He strode to the door and grabbed the knob. "You're not even trying to help me! I got the dope and I'm going to put somebody in jail for it! I'd sooner it be the pusher you got it from, but if I can't find him, you're the next best thing, you see?"

I did. With an icy clarity. Every crime had to have a criminal. It kept the books neat. Naively, I had assumed that everybody would get off if I could convince Sgt. Johnson of our innocent intentions, but the full implications of my choice grew terribly apparent as he waited for me to make up my mind, hand on the doorknob. It was hard to believe there wasn't an alternative to telling the truth. His glare of contempt chilled my spine; I couldn't meet his gaze.

"Well, come on, son! You still claim you found it?" he huffed. "You gonna sit there and tell me a white kid supplied a nigger musician with dope he'd never seen before?"

He kept staring at me. My jaw dropped a bit and my teeth parted as though I were about to speak, but what I'd say even I didn't know. My chin trembled; I shut my jaws and swallowed hard. I shivered again and let it stand as a shrug.

"Lord love a duck!" he spat and opened the door. "Bud?" he yelled down the hall. There was a distant "Yah?" then Sgt. Johnson roared, "Come get this silly sumbitch out of my sight! Lock him up!"

He left the door ajar and strode back to the desk, refusing to look at me. He yanked the top drawer open and tossed a pad and pencil into it, then straightened out the objects on the desktop: everything was final. Wait! God! What'd he want to know? That Terry and I had asked Stoogie for a few joints to tide us over for the long drive to Boston in a few days? That Stoogie had given it to us? But they'd believe that Stoogie had passed out free samples to get us hooked. Stoogie was a poverty-stricken musician who'd paid heavy dues and who could play alto in a way that could make your heart sing! He wasn't a dope peddler! Was he? How could I be sure enough that I'd gamble twenty years of my life on it?

Bud's footsteps had grown to monstrous explosions in the hallway. When it came time to sign on the bottom line, how could I lie? Wasn't that perjury? Didn't lies always get caught in the courtroom, even ones told with good intentions? And wouldn't I be piling trouble onto trouble by lying? I started shaking violently. I didn't want to go to jail! All my dreams. . . Bud's shadow fell across me when he walked through the door, and I blurted out that I hadn't found the stuff.

Later, I waited on one of the wooden benches outside the doors to the magistrate courtroom. My father wasn't thrilled to be awakened in the middle of the night to be told his son had been experimenting with narcotics and was at the police station where he could be released to his custody without charges filed. I dreaded the ride home.

But I was more relieved than anything else, and I could take his anger as easy payment for my guilt. I'd told them not only the facts, which they were happy to hear, but also the truth, which they weren't concerned about. They didn't care that I had *asked* Stoogie for the stuff, that he hadn't offered it. I kept insisting that we were all innocent in the sense that Stoogie and I and Terry were three musicians, friends, fellow craftsmen sharing a common pursuit, engaged in making jazz, and there was nothing any more sinister in our smoking joints than if "Bud" shared a beer with Sgt. Johnson in his living room. Sgt. Johnson pointed out that it was legal for him to drink beer in his living room.

I hadn't told him about Stoogie's stash at the golf course, narrowing my confession to what happened earlier in the night. I didn't know that Terry had told the same story more or less; I didn't know that Stoogie had clammed up, that in time they'd run a check and discover his first offense jail term. I only knew I was off the hook; even if I had to come back for a hearing or a trial, I wouldn't go to jail — my age, my parents, and my white skin had spared me that. With our horns, our high school diplomas, and our tuition fees, Terry and I could proceed as planned to become players of and at jazz, props and accouterments intact, while Stoogie would serve another sentence, this one longer than the first; he'd be stripped of everything he needed to play except the only thing they couldn't take, the thing they'd unintentionally give him — the suffering, the soul, the reason for the blues.

The beret in my pocket pressed like a fist into the cheek of my ass. I pulled it out and absently brushed out the wrinkles in the black felt and was about to put it on my head when my arms failed me and I dropped it to the bench. Directly across the hall the varnished courtroom doors gave off a dull gleam.

My gaze went to the ceiling light, then to the figure in bronze relief it illuminated just above the door: it was the same image I'd idly skimmed day after day on the textbook of the civics course I'd shown such promise in — Lady Justice in her robe holding up the level, empty scales, seeing nothing through her blindfold.

Letter
from the
Horse
Latitudes

Dad, your visit and our parting have stirred up things I'd long since hoped were still for good. Your every gesture spoke a need to ask how I came to be who and where I am.

Yet I can remember you as a fugitive. Garner State Park, Texas. We heard on the car radio the police were after you. I was eleven, thrilled to be in the company of a criminal. You who obey all laws great and small, you were deaf to the voice of Authority, fleeing the scene while Mother urged you to turn yourself in. You were (are) a lean man gnawed with American worry, quenching the fire in your gut with buttermilk and Bach, a virtuoso on your major talent — joking your way clear of painful situations.

"Calling all cars!" you boomed.

I laughed uproariously, delighted. *Who was that masked man?* My flattopped head was stuffed with what we left behind; some of those images lingered there for these many years, counting up to this afternoon.

No doubt a first for you, being pursued by the police. I recall when you became Scoutmaster for Troop #108, which met in the basement of the First Methodist Church on Tuesday nights. We were uneasy about the change; to meetings your predecessor had worn the suit he sold life insurance in, but you donned a Scoutmaster's uniform, complete with hat and kerchief. I was tormented that you were much too earnest, when I knew you privately to be a joker. Your religious air was deadly to our spirits. You never cursed, though this was consistent with your behavior at home. Your predecessor ribbed us about the manual's stern warnings to sleep with our hands above the covers, not to lie abed in the mornings, and to take cold showers when we felt "restless." He taught us the expression "loping your mule." We liked him; he knew who we were.

But you seemed oblivious to this side of our nature. At camp you strolled about at night leaving fruity wisps of pipe tobacco hanging in the air as you oversaw everything with the myopia we have in common, the least of many flaws that bind us. What's going on in the tents of the Phantom Buffalo Patrol is better left unacknowledged. Tonight, we "Phantom Butt-holes," as we're known, are trying to live down our name in a marathon farting contest. After lights are out and you've retired, we scoot out to other tents, stumbling onto cornhole orgies, barging in where the victor of a circle-jerk is sweeping up his winnings. The Explorers smoke Luckies on the sly, talk about getting your finger in it, heady stuff to us Phantom Buttholes. Behind the law, life goes on. A dangerous freedom crackles in the air, but you are asleep already.

It's not likely you've forgotten how proud I did you on the rifle range, but let me tell you why: for one, I take instruction exceedingly well; for another, what I saw in the targets helped. The Scoutmasters gathered just behind me on the firing line talked about Korea, where things hadn't gone well since "Frozen Chosin." I was paying close attention, having filled two scrapbooks with AP wirephotos and traced undulations of the battlelines on a map. Although I was only twelve, I'd heard Mother wish that the war would be over before I got older. She had good reason to fear: my secret ambition was to be the next Audie Murphy. Gradually, the conversation turned on the axis of collective guilt, and you all began trading credentials from the Big One. Last in line, you chuckled and told these bombardiers and dogfaces about your draft-exempt job in the oil fields, how with the "Home Guard" you went to the beaches to drill by tossing beer cans filled with sand into the surf, and the closest your unit came to danger was when a German sub was alleged to have surfaced five miles out in the Gulf from Galveston. You made no pretense that you would have preferred the thick of things — no, you made a joke of yourself, and even though they accepted you that way, I shut my eyes and concentrated on my target. The bull's-eye was a yellow head with slanting eyes. I sent many a round cracking up its nostrils and at the end of the day I won a plaque. My best shooting was from the sitting position, where I was calm, rock-steady in my aim because the sling was wrapped around my left forearm. The tautness of it was sensual, strangely comfortable, and familiar. This was the arm I wrapped my security blanket about as a child.

The armies I've belonged to! I'm thinking now of the rag-taggle corps of my neighborhood's ten-year-olds. We made wooden "longjohn" pistols and fired loops of rubber that left a satisfactory welt on a victim's arm or cheek; we made derringers out of clothespins and shot matchheads which burst into flame. Lucky souls got BB or pellet guns for Christmas or birthdays.

Saturday mornings we biked down to the Army Surplus store where the Big One's debris lay in musty heaps: helmet liners, entrenching tools, canteens and covers, cartridge belts, and packs, and once a plexiglass waist-gunner's bubble we dragged home to place over a foxhole dug in the pasture, putting us over Hamburg with the Jerries at 12 o'clock high! The canteen I bought had an elongated crease in its flank made, I was sure, by a grazing bullet. I would take a swig of Kool Aid from it and think: *This belonged to a guy who got shot at! I wonder if he got killed?*

We acted out scenes from war movies. We were informal scholars of the genre: Marines Establish a Beachhead, Army Air Corps Raids German Ball-Bearing Plant, Dogfaces Confront Panzer Tanks, Crippled Sub Hides from Jap Destroyer, Aircraft Carrier Attacked by Kamakazis. By age eleven or twelve, my knowledge of military lore and nomenclature far outstripped that of any other subject. In my bedroom sky the Corsair, the Grumman Hellcat, and The Mustang twirled in perpetual dogfights on the ends of strings. Light and heavy cruisers, destroyers, and carriers waged battles on my dressertop. I read "war funny books." I drew elaborate battle scenes, sketching in the tracers — even then I knew that every fifth round fired by a .30 or .50 caliber machine gun lit up to show where you were firing.

Oh yes, and hand-to-hand combat. On our patio you are lying in the hammock President/General Eisenhower told you to buy to save us from a recession. Time for my boxing lesson. I've primed myself by looking at your Golden Gloves medals under glass in your bedroom. A lightweight but fast. The gloves were a birthday present; they are huge, ruddy beehives on the ends of my arms, but on your knots of fist they are taut as sausage skins. Up from the hammock, you discuss stances, hovering over me to guide my arms and legs. There's jabs and hooks and uppercuts and haymakers and not getting hit in the breadbasket; there's not telegraphing your punches, keeping your chin tucked into your shoulder, presenting only a thin, protected profile to your opponent, feinting and following through, and, of course, not hitting below the belt or in the clinches. We spar; you bloody my nose by intentional accident. But it's all right — two days later I'm able to pass it on: my playmate from across the street refuses to return to me the tack hammer that is his, and so we go at it in the street, me with my dukes in the proper place, flailing away joyously and connecting right and left. His mother screams from her stoop for us to stop fighting. Behind me, I hear you yell, "Aw, let 'em scrap!" I redouble my efforts until he runs home bawling and bleeding about his nose and mouth. I saunter up our walk, flipping the hammer from handle to head in my palm. You smile. (In high school I learned refinements such as carrying a roll of dimes in my fist, or adding "brass knucks" secretly turned out in metal shop.)

War was a vital activity requiring men to perform brave deeds for which they were rewarded by medals whose titles and appearances I knew, as well as the names of a good many of their recipients and the circumstances under which they'd been earned. When I rushed up from my foxhole to charge the machine-gun nest against suicidal odds, going "dow-dow-dow," and spraying the enemy with hot lead, a great tingling shot up and down my spine, and I knew this was how I would've acted in the Big One, and that soaring thrill of facing danger and being proved a man was the play's reward.

Korea passed. The Cold War kept on heating up. As I

passed into puberty, the simple thrill of killing turned into something more earnest, more urgent. We believed in God, but the Russians didn't. Or, rather, the leaders of the Russians didn't, but the people did and weren't allowed to say so. For this reason, we might have to kill them whether it was fun or not, like eating oatmeal.

You ushered me to church, where my head swam with hymns, prayers, and stories (many of battles), and so God and Country were knotted together. I learned to ask God to give America strength. Although the word was not present in my vocabulary, the notion lurked at the dark perimeter of the prayer — Fatherland. This was God the Father's land. Other property was condemned.

In backyards across the nation fallout shelters were hastily excavated; Civil Defense wardens were appointed and volunteers posted signs and packed emergency supplies. Weapons were swept from den walls and carried to shelters to be used not on the Russians, who would probably not appear in person, anyway, but on neighbors who tried to take refuge in shelters not their own. The Civil Air Patrol initiated plane spotting in a windblown observation tower constructed at the city park (a good 300 miles from the Gulf of Mexico), and two hours a week I scanned the sky with binoculars for that stray Russian plane which had crept under our radar screens.

In ROTC we marched in front of the high school carrying our mock M-1s, each dying to call cadence when we came near where the girls played softball. By my senior year I belonged to the squad that used real M-1s borrowed from the National Guard; we came onto the field at half-time in our white helmet liners and dress gloves to do flashy Queen Anne salutes. The crowds roared approval, and a fever shimmering in the air always told me we were primed and fit for cannon fodder.

Vietnam. You didn't know, Dad, how hard I tried to stall my graduation. I felt all the same confusions everyone did — this war wasn't like the others; all the heroic elements of the Big One had been turned inside-out, and now we were the Nazis rushing across Poland, the Japanese attacking Pearl Harbor. Weren't we? Yes? No?

I couldn't sort this out before the draft board called. Many of my friends joined the Peace Corps or were active in the anti-war movement. I took the path of least resistance. But I also let an old chimera loom up to play me for a fool. If I had to go, I was determined to be a grunt, to get to the front, and return to document the horrors of war — each condition part of the sentimental baggage I'd carted around from my matinee days.

Life with the USMC at San Diego was like life with the ROTC and the BSA with a dash of hate and death added like picante sauce. You might recall I wrote to you to make the standard recruit's complaints about the petty acts of discipline — scrubbing the concrete floor of our Quonset hut with toothbrushes in the middle of the night, duck-walking the five hundred yards to the mess hall — which our drill instructors inflicted upon us with the zeal of fraternity boys initiating their pledges, and my complaints could have been characterized as the perfunctory grievances of the pledge who fully expects to take his hard-won place on the permanent roll. The marching, the regimented schedule, the rifle (though by then the M-16 had replaced my beloved M-1), the uniforms, the orders, the inspections, the protocol — it was all familiar, all to be expected; I did well, took care never to be first or last and could have breezed right onto a plane for Nam were it not for an unexpected development.

The lectures annoyed me more and more. "Lessons in Communism" was taught by an aging gunnery sergeant with surely not more than a fourth-grade education who persisted in making one factual error after another when he actually stuck to the subject, and he habitually dragged up his experiences in Korea as proof of his generalizations: the gooks had diabolical means of brainwashing the hordes under their whip so that they were hypnotized into being fanatically dedicated and loyal, but it wasn't like our kind of loyalty — it was more like being drugged or hopped up. This sometimes made them difficult to kill or get information from; for example, once he and three others took this gook bitch out of a village and tried to get her to tell them about enemy troop movements, but she kept claiming she didn't know anything "even when we rammed a shovel handle up her cunt."

Maybe I should have written to you about that. Several times my left hand jumped like a fish in my lap from the old classroom reflex to place an objection, but aside from my fear of openly questioning him, how could I have untangled his thoughts or have made a comment which protocol would demand be a question ending with, "Sir?" This classroom situation was like none I had ever experienced — the pupils were receivers whose only permissible comment was that they didn't fully understand.

I squirmed a lot, and that affected my equanimity, the suspended judgment that had allowed me to join. Outside camp in the streets of the nation, others of my generation — some my friends, no doubt — were organizing to head us off at the pass before we could reach the terminals, lying down in the streets and on the railroad tracks. Our drill instructors' vocabularies had become enriched with newly coined epithets such as "long-haired hippie queers" and "pinko fuck-face." Coupled with more traditional curses such as "yellow bastard" and "spineless fucker," the result was frequently amusing combinations such as "yellow hippie fucker!" which, to my ear, rang like the name of an exotic eel. Emerson's famous question to Thoreau began to haunt me. Or Thoreau's answer, rather. In moments of levity, or when they wished to reward us with a compliment to our fitness, our DIs cracked jokes about how they longed to march us into a peace demonstration and put us to work scattering yellow hippie fuckers right and left, a prospect that gnawed at me at night. I could too easily picture a street scene, my friends on one side of the barricades, myself on the other.

Did I write you about the lesson in the grenade? I may have left out the most significant part. This occurred at Camp San Onofre in the dusty, barren hills outside San Diego. Early evening. The class was held in a natural amphitheatre lying in a valley between two ridges; three platoons of us sat in bleachers facing the waning sunlight that streamed over the top of the ridge before us and blanketed the bleachers.

Before the lecture, we were smoking, our bellies plump with chow; the day was nearly over, and an almost festive mood was about to descend on me; the bleachers hummed with small talk, grabass, and you might have thought we were about to see a movie. Our instructor was a portly black E-6 with a jocular manner who actually got a laugh or two from us before getting down to business. The new grenade, called the "M-4," (if memory serves me right) was, he said, a *deadly* weapon. Your old grenade (I knew it well — the old "pineapple" in those films and comics) threw out shrapnel from its cover when it burst, shrapnel of limited quantities and of a size which would kill instantly or cause a wound which could be easily repaired — the chunk of metal could be located quickly. Now, your M-4 grenade (here he smirked), your M-4 has a thick jacket of steel mesh, like layers of chicken wire, and when it explodes it embeds these small bits of wire into the meat and tissue and bloodstream where they burrow slowly through the body like parasites, killing just as well, but taking a lot longer to do it and requiring more persons to attend to the wounded while he's dying; therefore, it is a more effective weapon: it maims and debilitates, turning fatal only as the last step in a slow process.

"Beautiful, huh?" Silhouetted against the setting sun, he held up the grenade. "Now, what is this?"

Rousing from our indolence: "Uh, M-4 grenade, Sir!"

"What? Can't hear you!"

"M-4 grenade, Sir!" we rumbled, louder.

"And what is it?"

Some confusion — we can't recall our lines. "Ah . . . uh . . . deadly, Sir!"

"What does it DO?"

"Kills, Sir!"

"Can't hear you!"

"KILLS, SIR!"

Some tittering; he is biting back a grin, and we are grinning in return as we yell.

"All right! Once again — what does it DO?"

Screaming: "KILLLSSSSS, SSSIRRRR!"

An echo bounded down that valley between the ridges — *illls illls illlsss irr irr irr* — and in that golden light hazy with motes, the declining sun warm against my face at the tranquil end of day, full-bellied, grinning, yelling this harrowing chant, I felt my third eye open and pull back from the scene to show me two hundred beasts clad in green gathered upon a strange planet to yell a mad blood-cry in unison, chortling as they did, and I wondered: are we a crime against nature or the very expression of it?

This was psyching up; our instructor was our cheerleader, and we were hollering for blood, priming ourselves to do the letting. I really didn't fear dying (I was much too young to believe I could), but I saw I was on my way to killing, inching closer every day, every lesson in the techniques and psychology of it bringing me sidled alongside it. The hate they tried so hard to instill in me was working like the blinders to keep the horse from leaping out of its traces.

I'd presumed the men who led me would be worthy of being followed, would set an example for me to measure up to. But with one exception (Sgt. Lacey), the DIs were corrupt, venial men, coming around on payday to collect for "relief funds" which we knew were nonexistent except as euphemisms for their own welfare. They enjoyed their cruelty; they dealt out an arbitrary justice, following the rules when it was to their advantage, applying Kafkaesque interpretations when it wasn't; they were paranoid; they sought excuses to use their hands and feet on us. I had expected them to be hard to please (part of the glamour of the Marines was the acclaimed "toughness") but found them neurotically picayunish; I expected sternness and saw only rigid aggression.

Above all, I'd expected them to be self-disciplined, self-denying. But they hardly, if ever, denied themselves anything they denied us. They drank all the water they wished on long, dusty hikes and hitched rides on passing Jeeps. They were unintelligent men whose liberties were spent, by their own jocular admission, beating up "queers" and abusing whores and getting blind drunk.

No man exemplified this more than Sgt. Spores. In the years since, when I've talked about him I've usually gotten an indulgent but incredulous smile from my listener because the sadistic DI is a stock character in any bootcamp anecdote, dozens of which I too had heard before I joined. Spores fit the stereotype so well that at first I thought he was only playing a role, but later I came to believe that his part had become fused to his personality so that he could no longer separate them: the role itself drew on some inward rage that both channelled and fueled it. The cliché handed him a ready-made direction for all his fury.

Ramrod straight bearing? Hardly. Sgt. Spores was a skinny man whose terrible posture produced, in profile, the appearance of a thick snake clothed in military garb trying to stand on its tail. He had a misshapen head, wide at the top and compressing inward at the temples and rounding again at the bottoms of his jaws, like the body of a guitar. Thick wet red lips pursed perpetually like a sphincter; two eyes like metal buttons, shallow and lifeless, above which lay thin brows almost albino-blonde. Holder of a black belt in karate, or so he claimed. (Jesus, I hated him. Still do. Over twenty-five years later now, and my teeth grind as I write this.) Also said "I married me a gook and regretted it ever since." Had the habit of cupping his left hand like a ball glove and chopping its palm with a karate-rigid heel of his right, except when other targets were handy, such as telephone poles and the napes of our necks. He couldn't keep his hands off us, and these sadistic caresses came to be etched on my crawling flesh with nightmarish clarity: he loved to clamp your carotid artery between his thumb and index finger; he dug his digits under your collarbone; he jabbed your Adam's apple with a hand drawn up in a claw; he'd wrench your ear like a schoolmarm; he'd knee you in the thigh and give you a Charlie-horse; he'd knee you in the balls.

Like all other DIs, Spores played favorites, and the apple of his eye was "Private Asshole," a black kid from rural East Texas who must have stood on tip-toe to meet the heighth requirement and eaten sourdough laced with lead to come up to weight. Private Asshole, whose real name I've forgotten, was a jittery sort, and finding himself receiving so much of Sgt. Spores's attention didn't increase his self-confidence. He was singled out in orders: "I want those rifles cleaned by 1400 hours, and that means yours, too, Private Asshole!" Or "Smoking lamp's lit for one cigarette, except for you, Private Asshole." Pvt. A invariably had to run ten laps around the platoon to get his mail; his rifle never once passed inspection (nor his rack, foot locker, uniform); he always did twice our calisthenics, twice the distance we ran, and had to remain behind to stand at attention guarding our stacked rifles while we went in to chow, was then given five minutes to eat, etc.

Pvt. A had the eyes of a skittish colt, large, brown watery orbs set in a milk-blue jelly, and they flicked constantly like hyper-alert antenna. He hardly ever spoke, made no friends, received mail from a single source — his "Mama," whose letters revealed (A was made to read two aloud) that he hadn't finished high school and joined the service because he needed a job, the Marines because the Army recruiter had been out to lunch. He was the smallest of us, the quietest, probably the youngest (I doubted he was truly eighteen), certainly the blackest. He took this punishment from Spores with a barely muted desperation, and so with a greasy ease he came quickly to be our scapegoat, too. Insults did not rebound; punches were not returned. Hating Spores as we did, Pvt. A's role as ritual goat got us off his hook, even helped explain why Spores hated us: if only we could rid ourselves of A, then maybe Spores would get off our backs, we secretly thought. We had noticed (thanks to Spores's pointing it out) that A had two lefts of everything: hands, toes, fingers, thumbs — he always left-shoulderarmed to our right, left-faced alone, and persisted in lagging two out-of-steps behind his rank, marking us as raw boots when we longed to look like like vets as we were marched by the receiving barracks. And Spores would explain our collective punishment thus: "No letter-writing tonight, maggots! You can thank Pvt. Asshole for that!"

By the time we were to begin training at the rifle range, our platoon had shed its "ten-percenters," that statistical grouping of physical and psychological washouts: one broke a leg, one confessed to being homosexual, one had an outbreak of rheumatic fever, and one had recurring nightmares that woke us all with blood-chilling screams. "Ten-percenters" were pariahs ("ten-percenter" was as an epithet as scalding as "maggot" or "individual"), and, though Spores tried to place Private A in that category, A hung onto his place on the roster as we left for the range.

Meanwhile, Spores stressed the supreme necessity for each man to shoot a qualifying score with his rifle; there was no greater humiliation for a DI than to have a boot fail to qualify, nor was there a greater shame for the recruit. The Marine Corps wasn't like other branches of the service (which by implication were populated by cowards, morons, and perverts); in The Crotch even a cook learned to shoot properly and effectively.

Not to anyone's great surprise, Pvt. A was the only recruit in our platoon who did not qualify, due in no small part to the help Spores gave by standing over him with one boot planted on either side of his hips as he lay on the firing line, yelling as A jerked his trigger and sent round after round spewing dirt up in the butts and getting a red flag — "Maggie's drawers" — from his target-pullers. A last riddle in a self-fulfilling prophecy had been revealed; we were free to hate him, he who disqualified in our stead.

In saner moments, I could have untangled the dynamics of the whole wretched syndrome, beginning with Spores's bigotry and ending where it did, but I wasn't altogether in my right mind, and how I've worked to come back to it is a lot of what this letter is about. Then, though, I seethed with everybody else because Pvt. A had incurred Sgt. Spores's wrath on the lot of us, and we had to run back to tent camp from the rifle range at a port-arms doubletime. Sepulvida, running just behind A, kept kicking A's bony little ass as we huffed and panted through the hills in the dust and heat, dying for water and still three miles to a stop. We were supposed to have had a piss call before running back to camp, as we had been out on the range since just before noon without one, but Spores had denied it for obvious reaons, so many of us were suffering the maddening, paradoxical pangs of an aching bladder and a parched mouth. It's notable that Spores ran the whole way with us that afternoon, part of the syndrome being his need to feel that Pvt. A was punishing *him*, forcing him to run five miles in the heat and dust of a California summer afternoon. Therefore, Pvt. A would pay.

"I . . . said," Spores gasped when he had halted us in raggedy-assed formation outside our tents, "I wanted every one of you turds to qualify!" His chest heaved and sweat dripped off his jawline. "And you didn't. Fuckers!" He panted a moment, and we huffed with him. "Did I say you could piss your pants!!!" he bellowed suddenly, and in an instant was hovering over Pvt. A. "Did you hear me give you a pissing order!?"

I cast a sidelong glance. A large dark spot was spreading over Pvt. A's trousers. He was not alone — I spotted two others. I was about to go, too.

"No, Suh!"

"You fucking maggot!" The cuff to A's temple almost bowled him over, then he cried the first public words he had ever uttered in his own defense. "I couldn't help it, Suh!"

Spores writhed and trembled in speechless agitation in

front of him for a few seconds. He then turned and gave us all three minutes for a piss call (except for A, of course), and sixty-one of us dashed frantically for the eight toilets in the head, popping buttons as we ran and stampeding into the building, slung rifles clattering, bristling and jabbing; we pissed all over each other's boots and pants' legs then sprinted madly back into formation. A and Spores had vanished.

"At rest, you fuckers!" Spores yelled from inside the duty tent just behind us. "Water up. Lamp's lit for one cigarette."

Gratefully, we unhusked canteens and lit up, our bladders lax as old balloons. Unlike the order "Parade Rest," the position of "At Rest" allowed us to pivot about upon one stationary foot, the left. We were free to talk, and with A's fate now a private matter between him and Spores, we took leisurely drags off cigarettes and cooled down after the five-mile run. A low mumble arose as everyone tried to work their high scores into conversation or rationalize low ones.

"Shit maggot!" we heard from the duty tent behind us. There were titters in the formation: who gave a rat's ass if A was going to get another cussing?

"Nigger turd!"

A few snickers chirped up in the ranks above the general mumble. Ross pivoted around to look toward the duty tent and raised an eyebrow to me.

"What'd you shoot, man?"

We heard a low keening, like a continuous whimper.

"NIGGER MAGGOT!"

An idiotic fury erupted in Spores's voice; Ross and I almost burst into laughter to hear this insane gibberish of frustration, Spores's anger having stripped him of what was an already meagre imagination. Poor A, I thought.

"One twenty-eight," I said.

I was half-expecting Spores to carry the spare handful of grammatical components to its nonsensical conclusion with "shit turd!" but instead we heard a thump and a clatter, followed by a moan. Pivoting on my left foot, I saw the side of the duty tent pop outward driven by a round projectile I feared was A's head, then the canvas side fell slack, and we heard sobbing. One side wall of the duty tent had been rolled up for ventilation, and now we could see that A had fallen to the floor, the heel of one boot visible at the edge of the wooden deck the tent was pitched upon; the rest of the interior was dim, with vague green shapes in motion.

A curse was choked back, as though Spores had tried to shout but was strangling on his own phlegm, then I could make out a black shape in a swift arc that ended abruptly in a green form, and an "Oww! Uh!" as Spores's boot landed somewhere on A's body. Three more times, and each connection was a muffled *thut!* in the air.

A began crying, "Don't Suh! Please don't no more, Suh!"

Another flurry of blows. "Maa Maaa!" A's wailing penetrated our chatter like a siren.

"What'd ya get prone on the 500?" Ross was knocking on my arm to get my attention. He was nervous, his face flushed, squinting at me almost angrily.

"What?" I asked, confused. I kept twisting on my left foot to turn from his oddly agitated face to the duty tent where a clatter of overturning furniture told me Spores wasn't finished yet.

"I shot a forty-six," said Ross. "How about kneeling and sitting, what'd ya do?" He bobbed on his feet and spat toward the duty tent. We heard another cry of pain. "I got a forty-six!"

Looking down the ranks I saw that several others were

sending quick, nervous glances behind them toward the duty tent. A few were elbowing each other, grinning and gesturing furtively. Still the crashing, the muffled knocks, the cursing and the sobbing went on — I pictured Spores picking A up by his collar and tossing him around. If we weren't At Rest, I thought, I'd go in there and . . . what? I didn't know. My left foot was rooted in place, and I kept hobbling about in a circle like an animal with one paw caught in a trap.

At last all sound ceased from the tent.

"I . . . got a forty-four," I told Ross.

After a moment, Spores appeared in the doorway to his tent, sweating and serene. "Stack your rifles, wash up and get back in formation in ten minutes for chow," he said quietly.

We never saw Pvt. Asshole again; Spores kept him in the duty tent for the rest of the afternoon and evening, and when he got a chance, Pvt. A tried to go over the hill, collapsed outside of camp, was discovered by a family of civilians and returned to Sick Bay, where he was immediately operated on for a "burst appendix," according to reports filtering back to us.

During the remaining weeks of training I was plagued by recurring cameo memories: A's bootsole resting on the floor of the duty tent, a man plunging into a river. These images were flags, a semaphor of something gone wrong, though I didn't know it, then. Marching on, I ignored them. Now Spores and the platoon could hold our heads high; the record showed every recruit had qualified; the record showed that we had shed all our "ten-percenters." Now there was no essential difference between what Spores was and what we had become.

What happened to Pvt. Asshole? some brave soul ventured one night as we stood lighting up during the last smoking lamp of the day, encouraged by Spores's admission he was proud of us.

"Aw!" Spores spat. "That fucker couldn't even shine his shoes."

Later, we heard he would be court-martialed and given a Bad Conduct Discharge, when he healed. He had no business here. He was not one of us. (We had seen to that.) Wasn't he better off on the outside? Weren't we better off without him? Wasn't Spores happier? Weren't we more at ease?

Yes, to all accounts. There would always be that ten percent, so don't sweat it, I kept counselling myself, only to be answered by that image of A's boot, then the clip of a lean man with white skin surging into the water in his baggy boxer shorts. How these images were connected, I couldn't say.

I posed as proudly as any for the platoon's graduation picture and spent the morning strutting on the grinder before the admiring eyes of my fellow Marines' sisters and girlfriends, reliving the ancient ROTC urge for display, the glamour of it a reward for those weeks of struggle.

But the bubble burst the minute I stepped onto the plane for home. I was afraid that alone I would utter something to myself I didn't want to hear, and I longed to be back with the platoon, to be reassured that the process that had produced what I had become was a legitimate and healthy undertaking for human beings.

"Welcome home, killer!" Thus, grinning, you greeted me as I walked into the terminal, jabbing me lightly and affectionately on my shoulder. My uniform impressed you, made you proud, but my blush was not from modesty. Nor was it modesty that kept me from putting the uniform back on again once I had changed into civvies. Clothes.

I wanted to tell you something then, but I didn't know

how to say it and wouldn't for several years, wouldn't, really, until our meeting this week. Two and a half decades is a long time to avoid a subject, I know. My silence even seems *historic*, somehow; it began in '64 when I became a fugitive here and kept on even after I'd been "pardoned" by Carter, and continued even after you'd relented and come to visit.

If you'd asked me then, eons ago during that leave, if something were bothering me, I could have only said I was carrying two pictures in my head but didn't see how they were related. You didn't ask; I didn't volunteer. Instead, I spent two weeks spinning yarns, letting legends substitute for what I really had to say, hiding behind the aura of "Marine" as you introduced me around your office. I experienced a wave of nausea on being shown the clipping from our local paper in which I appeared in my helmet, a grim tuck to my lips appropriate for one undergoing the rigors of learning to kill. Awkward moments arose when the TV showed protesting students going limp or being tear-gassed; people would try to coax a fang-baring from me, but I clammed up in silences that were misread as slow burns.

I've always been glad I took the hard way back to California; it's as if I unconsciously knew I had something to work out and my mind produced the eighteen-hour bus trip as a hiatus for it. Near El Paso, my fingernails were tiny particles suspended in my saliva. Germany, all those thousands silent while the ovens burned. (Oh, come on! Don't be melodramatic!) Still, why hadn't I done something? (Such as?) Such as stopping Spores from beating A. (But you couldn't, you know? You were "At Rest"; one foot belonged to you, but the other had been planted in place by the order, and you couldn't very well go into the duty tent without lifting your left foot, even if the right was free to go. Nobody else did anything, either. A's fate was inevitable; he was a ten-percenter.)

Phoenix. I twisted and turned in my seat and butted my head against the window of the bus. My conscience didn't care that no one else had acted, and as for A's "fate," it was one thing to tell a man he isn't suited for the Corps, give him his papers and a ticket for home, and quite another to bedevil him for thirteen weeks until he cannot perform, kick him repeatedly in the ribs, stomach and back until an organ ruptures, then toss him out with a BCD (but you couldn't move that left foot, you know —).

What, was it staked to the sand? Was I in leg irons?

Before the bus reached Barstow, I got the shakes; at 2:00 A.M. the desert was a refrigerated plain illuminated by a full moon's bony light. The claims my culture had made on me seemed overwhelming, and I felt I had been tooled on an assembly line. I thought when I got back I would report what Spores had done to the company's commanding officer or to my congressman. Then I worried that, back among them all, their control over my mind would be reasserted and I'd be argued out of it. That left foot *was* indeed staked to the sand, I saw, and that stake was in my mind. Too much of me belonged to them, too much of me was part of the mob.

I got off the bus at Barstow and stewed around inside the depot hoping to make little acts of dawdling constitute a larger choice. Sipped a Coke, trembling, then at the last minute before time to depart for L.A., I got the driver to abort my sea bag from the belly of the bus and stood on the curb watching the vaporous spume of diesel-wash obscure its taillights as it swept on west without me.

How I remember your first visit here five years after that. "Nobody knows how things will turn out," you mused, puffing on your pipe. Turning to peer at you as we strolled down the earthen path to see the new piglets and the calf, I was a little surprised to discover I'm taller and heavier than you. Your smile was bemused; your comment was inspired by the disorientation of your long plane ride and the tangible reality of my life as a part-time teacher and farmer here on the Saskatchewan plain, living in "sin" with a woman and fathering a child not my own who might as well have been dropped on my stoop by gypsies (though he's your grandson, should you choose to think so).

Later, while Mother and Betsy skirmished politely in the kitchen, we sat in my study (at least, this is my memory of it), you on your second beer and I on my eighth, your eyes taking embarrassed probes at my props, my early '70s icons: posters of Uncle Sam with his middle finger waggling obscenely, of a nude woman in a provocative pose, of a giant marijuana leaf. Book covers implied that my heroes were now insane black men who brandish machine guns and Maoism; other texts whispered of drug-lunacy, rituals of hallucination and mysticism. Conspicuously absent were the sorts of text which guided our ancestors — Confederate army officers, plantation owners, merchants, mayors, bond brokers, realtors — on their trek to prosperity and posterity: your Bibles, your Boy Scout handbooks, the *Wall Street Journal.*

We groped at small talk, batted about the lives of my high school classmates; I inquired desultorily about them, and you supplied the information, rather wistfully I might add, that for the most part they were careered, married, childrened, moving upward in institutional echelons, arguing cases, curing diseases.

"What about Ron McLaughlin?" I asked.

"He's dead," you said. You might remember there was an abrupt silence, then you blurted out: "He got killed in Vietnam." Oh Christ! A flash of anger shot out before you could check it — don't deny it! — indignation, really: *now* wasn't I sorry I didn't go? Or maybe for an instant you thought it was my fault he was killed because I wasn't there to help him. Didn't "support" him by believing the war was justified. But then I watched your face contort and sweep through different phases, struggling to return to neutrality: you saw at once how absurd and terrible it was to wish Ron's fate on me, and I saw how readily you would have and burst into laughter, at the absurdity of our cross purposes, at our embarrassment. I hope you didn't regret it that after a minute you began to chuckle also, despite your wish to keep a grave face out of respect to the dead.

Then we simply dropped the subject for another twenty years. You know how these things go: it's not that time makes it easier to be silent; it makes it harder to speak.

But yesterday, I sensed we were ready to talk. I'm grateful you brought up the business about my great-great-grandfather, Tyrone, not only because it revealed you had been parting the branches of the family tree to find some precedent to justify me, but because it led me to this business about yourself as a fugitive. Yes, I did remember that Tyrone was an officer in the military escort that marched the Cherokees from Georgia to Oklahoma on the famous Trail of Tears, and I also recall that afterward he refused "every dime" of his pension. You wanted to be as proud of that act of conscience as you were of me in my uniform; you wanted to be proud of my reasons for "desertion," but you weren't certain you could be. Though a glimmer of mirth played in your eyes, the sadness dragged at your mouth, the skin along your jaw hung loose, and I could almost hear you think: Such a fine shot! Such good grades! And an Eagle Scout!

You didn't tell the rest of the story, either because you'd forgotten it or because you didn't want to remind me that, conscience-stricken as old Tyrone was, when they reached the end of that Trail of Tears he dashed right back to

Georgia to stake a claim on a sizeable portion of the land he had just run the Cherokees off of, so he had more to atone for than was indicated in your tale. What his story says is that his conscience was strong enough to irritate but not reform him. Giving up that pension? An empty gesture.

But I felt a kinship with old Tyrone. I knew then why I'd never talked with you about my going over the hill. I secretly feared I might discover my reason wasn't as sound as I'd hoped. In those earlier years here, when you came to visit, I was playing the exile; I was an expatriate who had left AmeriKa because it wanted me to kill Third World peasants in a senseless war. Now, another decade and a half later, my own history has suffered revisionism. I came to Canada in an effort to dignify two successive failures: the failure to help poor Pvt. A and the subsequent failure to return to the ranks and right the wrong done him. Refusing to serve and going AWOL were far less honorable than either of those alternatives, but not, perhaps, dishonorable. By coming here I could pretend for many years that my refusal to serve was an act of courage and conviction. Now I think that it was simply the best of the bad solutions; now I try to put the best face on it — A did not die in Vietnam, and I killed no one there.

On the way to the airport, I thought of trading your story about Tyrone for one of my own, about how Magellan, pursued by the Spanish armada, led his own fleet into the Horse Latitudes because he knew that no sailor in his right mind would deliberately veer off into that vast water-desert barren of wind, and so he escaped from the armada, whose captains never thought to look there. But in the meantime, he won the contempt and wrath of the captains and crew of every vessel under his command. I intended to leave you that to chew on for a few years; time robbed me of a chance to tell it, and, much more importantly, it happened that the memory of your fleeing the scene at Garner State Park rushed back to me as your plane lifted off the runway at Regina and my arm flew up in a reflex to call you back to remind you of it.

Sheets of water from the morning's rain, still as ice to the eye, spread across the runway after your plane was a tiny segment of line in a darkening sky, and I stood at the wire with that memory burning like a vision to weld my world together. You should have known better than to blame me for my choice, you who would have felt the same, patriot or no. I even suspect you might have gone one better — maybe stopped Spores, reported him.

We stood on the river bank with mouths agape and hearts in our throats as the child, breathless and hysterical, screamed, "My Daddy's drowning!" waving madly at the clear expanse of river to our front which was smooth and unbroken but for a few ripples carrying a cluster of bubbles. The child's banshee wail and his dervish dance undid us all, adults and children alike, and everyone began hopping on the pebbly beach as if hot-footed. In all honesty I can't say that "without a second's hesitation" you dove into the water, because your first motion seemed convulsive, like a gigantic, coordinated spasm, then you whirled as though unsure of where to go or as if you expected to see someone official go whizzing into the water, but no one did, so you kicked off your shoes and shed your trousers and ran into the river in your sock feet, the water surging around your knees, then plunged forward into the deep green pool where the man had disappeared.

We waited; after a long, tense pause, you rose for a huge gasp of air, vanished again. Then you brought the man up, dragged him out onto the bank and gave artificial respiration the old way, with him prone and you astraddle his hips, your palms pressing his ribcage. Finally, he coughed up water, came to.

Who was that masked man? We eased away under cover of noisy whoops of relief from the man's family and slipped off to our campsite, stowed away our gear and drove off before anyone could get your name. Perhaps you would've gotten an award; as a kid I read a book about Carnegie medal winners and was thrilled to think that but for your modesty, you'd have been in it, too.

What I saw too late yesterday as our hands broke apart and you were moving toward your plane with your lean American's worried walk was that we are two idealists squinting at one another across a chasm of American history, alike in more than just our myopia. The gap which separates us is not our difference, but, paradoxically, our likeness: you taught me that the drowning should be saved.

Hugo Molder
and the
Symbol of Displaced
Persons Everywhere

*H*ugo Molder's Gas & Grocery sat next to a weedy, mesquite-choked pasture vacant but for an eight-foot concrete statue of an Indian bearing the words "Srs. '73" in crude black letters across its belly. The statue was to have been donated to the State of New Mexico by an old widow, who hadn't intended for it to stay in the lot, although Hugo didn't know that. She told the workmen to set it down there until she could find a permanent place for it, but she died before she got around to it. Travelers who stopped for gas at Hugo's usually asked how it came to be there.

Hugo Molder had a false front tooth that he used like a valve to let air into his mouth while he pursed his lips in thought. When someone asked about the Indian, he'd push the bottom of the tooth out with the tip of his tongue, suck air through the hole, and gaze over at his son, Weldon.

Weldon Molder was eighteen and, according to Hugo, had lifted a calf daily from its birth until it became a year-ling. When Weldon wasn't lifting calves or lounging in the bleachers at the Oil City swimming pool, he liked to sit just inside the door to Hugo's place atop a Coke case propped against the wall, spitting between his feet and cleaning his fingernails with the switchblade he brought back from his senior trip to Juarez, leaning there listening to the cars approach the light at the crossroads just outside. Weldon always bragged he could tell by the sound alone whose car had pulled up to the light. He'd shield his eyes with one hand, wave the other in front of him to shush anyone who might be wanting to tell him the answer, and then he'd yell, "Lowe's little Gimmy!" or "Jackie Ray's 'Cuda!"

But when Hugo flicked his tooth and looked over at him when people asked about the statue, Weldon would chuckle and slap his thigh as if to say it never failed that somebody asked that.

Hugo had an answer. He'd furrow his brow, flip his tooth, suck air, wait for Weldon to slap his thigh, then he'd answer, "You know, lots of folks ast that," bobbing his head curtly. Oddly enough, people seemed to think this answered the question. At least, no one had ever followed up with "and what do you tell them?" perhaps because Hugo's answer seemed to say that since lot of folks had asked, he had given out lots of answers; therefore, it was no longer a mystery.

Hugo was asked the question one day by Harvey Gubberman, a foundation garment salesman on his way home to Dallas after tending to his new territory in western New Mexico. A former New Yorker who liked to spend his evenings in his motel rooms increasing his word power or taking personality tests he found in mass circulation magazines, Gubberman had noticed the statue the last time he had driven by. When he braked and pulled onto the shoulder to take a slower look at it, a phrase — "symbol of displaced persons everywhere" — popped to mind for no apparent reason. An odd thought, he thought, as he didn't have many along this line, but it pleased him enough that he wrote a note about it and placed it in his wallet next to the six-year-old slip of notebook paper folded in sixteenths on which he had written a few lines of rhymed verse on the occasion of his firstborn's bar mitzvah.

Despite his disinclination to frequent places which looked as though they might contain persons who sat just inside the door on Coke cases cleaning their fingernails with switchblades, on his return through he decided to inquire about the statue and get something cold and wet to drink. He was very thirsty from driving six hours with a hangover (a business drinker only, he had been obliged to attend a buyers' gathering the previous evening) and from coming down off of diet pills he'd borrowed from his wife for his long drives.

As he waited for Hugo to answer his question about the statue, he searched the battered red sides of the Coke cooler box for an opener so he could quench his thirst with the ice cold Pepsi that was sweating profusely, marvelously, in his hand. Not finding one, he decided to insert a parenthetical question into the midst of Hugo's contemplation about the statue's origin.

"Have you got an opener?" he asked before Hugo could answer, "Lots of folks ast that," or "You know, lots of folks been asking that." Hugo had been trying to select between those two when Gubberman asked his second question.

Hugo had heard the second question many times, too; it was the middle question in a set of three. Usually he'd reach out for the customer's soft drink, swing his arm over to the cash register for a screwdriver he kept on the ledge above the drawer, and then he'd hoist his hammy buttocks up onto the Coke cooler at the end above the seldom-selected lime and strawberry sodas, just across the door from Weldon, insert the bottle between his thighs, grasp the neck in his left hand and pry off the cap with the screwdriver blade.

Hugo considered this an extra little service he rendered to his customers, something to bring them back again, like the station attendants in the big cities who used to sweep out floorboards and check the fluid levels. He had considered charging a quarter for it, having said to himself one day in irritation that he'd like to have a quarter for every time he'd had to open one that way, but in the long run he enjoyed feeling generous for not charging. Hugo didn't know that was why he didn't get an opener, but his answer to the third question indicated it.

After he had been at work only a short while on the Gubberman's bottlecap, he grew aware that the salesman was shifting his weight from foot to foot. He didn't let it hurry him, though, because the best things took a little longer, but Gubberman, whose favorite spectator sport was watching his teenage sons play table tennis, finally asked, with a touch of annoyance he tried to conceal, why Hugo didn't get himself a bottle opener.

This was the third question. Like his answer to the first, Hugo's answer to the third didn't explain much, but people thought it did. He'd screw up his brow, flick his tooth out, and say in mock surprise, almost as though it was entirely beyond him what that Hugo Molder was up to, "You know, I don't know!" and shake his head sadly. This answer also discouraged a follow-up; it implied that the ultimate answer couldn't be known because the fellow who might know it wasn't around.

But the third question threw Hugo's rhythm off; dimly, he knew that *Why's that statue there? Do you have an opener? Why not?* had been asked in their normal sequence though more quickly than usual, and so, like an expert called in to make a judicious decision, he pondered a while on which to answer first. While Gubberman was mopping his brow and mooning at the still unopened Pepsi, upon which work had temporarily been suspended, Hugo finally decided to address them in chronological order.

"You know, lots of folks ast me that," he said to clear up the mystery about the statue of the Indian in the next-door lot.

"What do you tell them?" Gubberman wondered aloud, curious as to why he was having to undergo the torture of watching Hugo take five minutes to open the cap of an icy Pepsi he had been yearning lustily for the last fifty-seven miles in the 100-degree heat after a breakfast of two cups of black coffee and thirteen cigarettes.

Hugo's tooth jutted out suddenly.

"Jackie Ray's 'Cuda!" Weldon screamed, then spat beside his boots. Startled, Gubberman jumped; Hugo, anxious for the welfare of his customer, decided that before he'd answer the salesman's third question about the opener, he'd try to explain why Weldon, after throwing out one arm and shielding his eyes with one hand, should for no reason shout a name. He looked at Gubberman.

"Just a hobby," he said.

Cockamamie country smartass, thought Gubberman, feeling his tongue writhe convulsively for a drink. Images of oceans sloshed and slapped in his head. But rather than demand that Hugo practice his peculiar hobby in the privacy of his own home and relinquish the Pepsi so he could tear the lid off with his teeth, he decided a drink of water might keep him from going stark raving mad while Hugo tinkered like a Swiss watchmaker with the bottlecap.

"Where's your water fountain?"

Hugo didn't hear him; he was still clearing a path back through the other two questions. Part of his mind stored Gubberman's fourth question away so he could come to it after the third, on which he was presently at work, the second having been answered in effect when he took the bottle, and so, reaching the third question regarding the opener, he jabbed his tooth out twice, winked and said, as though it struck *him* strange, too, "You know, I don't know!"

With some uneasiness Gubberman deduced that if Hugo didn't know where the fountain was, then he didn't really belong there. Watching Hugo's peculiar leer, the tooth flip back and forth, he had a sudden vision of the store's rightful proprietor lying in the back room bound and gagged by two assailants, both escapees from a mental hospital, one a chunky redheaded man who was opening a bottle with a screwdriver so he'd have a weapon handy, and had positioned himself on one side of the door, and the other a strapping teenage maniac who sat across from him, effectively blocking any exit. He tried to shake off this sinister vision by looking at Hugo as if to ask for a reasonable explanation of why he didn't know the location of the water fountain.

"I just don't know," Hugo repeated, leering and wagging his head to and fro in wonder. Then he returned to the bottle and tried to recall Gubberman's fourth question.

"I guess you're new here?" Gubberman asked hopefully in a phlegm-choked voice.

"Bubba Redfearn's Chevy-smasher!" Weldon hollered and looked at Hugo for confirmation. Hugo glanced out the door.

"Nope." Hugo smiled as if to say they couldn't expect him to get it right every time, could they?

Weldon sighed, leaned against the wall, slid his hand into his Levis pocket and extracted his switchblade, snapped it open and began cleaning his fingernails. Gubberman, whose impressions about what happened to strangers who hung around little country towns were rather definite, if not graphic, grew curious about a rear exit. Because he couldn't go out the front door with Hugo and Weldon on either side, he tried to imagine he was only imagining things, but he saw nothing benign in Weldon's smirk. He and the other man seemed to be waiting for something, to be timing something — perhaps a third man was in the rear, looting a safe? Gritting his teeth, feeling his nerves scrape like chalk against the blackboard of his body, he tried to shake off the notion by telling himself he'd been up too long.

Meanwhile, Hugo had reached the fourth question. Not many people asked him about the fountain because it was attached to the end of the coke cooler in plain sight when Hugo wasn't sitting on top of that end. He didn't have a ready answer. His dilemma was further complicated because the fountain hadn't worked in six months. He held a practice conversation in his head with the salesman concerning the fountain; he told him its location, remembered it wasn't working, so he had to tell him that, too; however, he saw he could shorten his answer by simply saying the fountain was out of order. In the meantime, he had eased the lid off the bottle and as he thought out his answer he found himself staring at the Pepsi in his hand. The open bottle was a new development. He now realized that Gubberman had wanted a drink of water to hold him until he got his Pepsi, but now he could have the Pepsi and didn't need the water, thus he didn't need to know either the fountain's location or condition.

He held the bottle up, vaulted off the top of the Coke

cooler and lunged toward Gubberman, waving the screw-driver wildly.

"You won't be needing it now!" he chortled.

Gubberman took a quick step backward and raised his hands. "Please don't," he blurted out.

Puzzled, Hugo paused in mid-stride, holding out the bottle to Gubberman, who blushed when he saw that Hugo had no more diabolical act in mind that handing him the Pepsi; Gubberman chided himself and struggled to keep his delinquent imagination in check. Taking the prof-fered bottle, he mumbled thanks, upended the Pepsi and would have chugalugged the contents had he not foreseen that one wouldn't satisfy his thirst that way and he couldn't endure Hugo's opening another. Relieved, his sanity restored by the Pepsi's cold reality cascading down his throat, his curiosity about the statue returned. Perhaps some friendly chatter would prompt Hugo to explain it.

"I guess this really is your place?" he asked weakly. Odd way to phrase it, he thought. He had only meant to ask if Hugo was the proprietor.

Hugo eyed him closely now that opening the bottle had freed his capacity to concentrate. When you got right down to it, the man was a weird bird, what with asking all sorts of questions one right after the other and never waiting for an answer, saying strange things when Hugo handed him his bottle. He was just too curious. Hugo recalled that the man hadn't bought any gas; as he stared long and hard and deep at Gubberman, noting his bloodshot eyes, the tic jumping across his cheek like a frog's leg in a frying pan, his nervous shuffling from one foot to the other, he sized the man up to be one of three things — an escapee from an insane asylum, a dope addict, or a thief. Then, with some horror, he realized that the three categories weren't mutu-ally exclusive.

Hugo had been robbed three times in the past five years and he was so sick and tired of it that after the last time he and Weldon had worked out a plan to use in case they had any chance of preventing it. He tried to recall the code to set the plan in motion, which called for Weldon to get behind the robber to distract him long enough for Hugo to pull his shotgun out from under the counter.

"What's that you say?" Hugo asked slyly, holding his hand to his ear as if he were deaf. "You say something about Geronimo?"

Strange, Gubberman thought. He hadn't said anything remotely resembling the word "Geronimo." Was that their name for the statue?

"I said," he began, about to repeat his previous question verbatim but recalled that the original phrasing had been eccentric. "I said is this your place?"

"You *betcha*!" Hugo declared.

Gubberman ducked Hugo's glare by lifting the bottle and letting the cola into his mouth in little spurts. Weird, he thought. Worried, he inhaled deeply and encouraged himself to think of the whole experience as something he had blown up in his mind, that these two people were only humans like himself with predictable patterns he might come to know and love(?) were he around long enough to discern and explain them. He vowed that no matter what else occurred, he wasn't going to be swayed into thinking they were out to get him, because that was just plain paranoia, pure and simple.

Just as Gubberman made his vow, Weldon received Hugo's message about Geronimo and looked up to see Hugo glaring at the stranger. He swung into action; whistling loudly to suggest nonchalance, he yawned, stretched hugely, then rose from the Coke case and continued to clean his fingernails, standing with his feet wide apart for greater balance in case he had to made a sudden move. Then, humming, he edged sideways like a crab, very, very slowly, moving exactly like someone who doesn't want it to be known he's moving. Gubberman clenched his eyes shut so he couldn't watch it. I did not see that man move that way, he told himself as he finished the Pepsi. He thought of telling them what he'd been thinking, telling it to them like a joke — then they could reassure him and everybody'd laugh and his fears would be dispelled and maybe he could even find out about the Indian. He knew it was going to sound crazy, but he desperately needed objective confirmation.

"I know this sounds awfully silly," he ventured to Hugo, chuckling as he set the empty bottle on the counter. "I'm a little ashamed to admit it because it sounds so strange, but do you know for a minute there I thought you two were some kind of robbers or killers?" He laughed hoarsely, croaking.

"What made you think a thing like that?" Hugo guffawed mightily as he drew the shotgun from behind the counter and nodded to Weldon, who pressed the point of his switchblade into Gubberman's back.

Gubberman fainted.

He awoke on the floor, his hands and feet bound with fishing line. Hugo was seated backwards in a cane bottom chair aiming the shotgun at his face. Weldon snickered beside him, holding the point of his knifeblade up to show him that if the shotgun didn't rip his head clean off, the knife'd slash him to ribbons. The instant he tried to speak, Hugo jerked the shotgun to his shoulder.

"You move a muscle or say anything at all and there won't be nothing left of you but a little greasy spot," he snarled. Gubberman shuddered at the image.

The second the sheriff came in and spoke to Hugo,

Gubberman saw what the mistake had been, but as he tried to explain it to the sheriff, the highway patrolman who had come in with him was searching his car and found the empty bottle of his wife's diet pills. Gubberman had taken the last five dexamils out of the bottle the previous evening and put them in his shirt pocket, knowing that, considering his exhaustion and the distance he had to drive, he'd probably take them all eventually. He had taken three since then.

Being afraid the sheriff wouldn't understand and that they might hang a drug rap on him by mistake, Gubberman surreptitiously fished the last two tablets out of his pocket and swallowed them, thereby eliminating, as it were, the evidence. He was seated in the back seat of the sheriff's car when this took place. The sheriff kept holding the empty bottle up. Now where did you get this? he asked for the fifth time.

"It's my wife's," Gubberman responded patiently. "Why don't you call and ask?"

The sheriff chuckled as if to say he never ceased to be amazed.

Meanwhile, Hugo and Weldon and the patrolman stood off to the rear of the sheriff's car.

"Hell, I knowed he was a dope fiend the minute he come in the door," Hugo was saying. "Kept shifting from one foot to the other."

"Huh!" the patrolman exclaimed. He had enjoyed hearing about how the plan had actually worked to catch the man. Hugo had explained to him how each part of the code had originated and grown through a logic all its own. The deaf part told Weldon to listen up and the Geronimo part told him to jump into action because there was a thief (Indian) around, but jump in carefully, like an Indian. The patrolman nodded. He admired the plan because to an innocent passerby Hugo would only appear to be doing something quite natural, holding his hand behind his ear and pretending to be deaf while he asked what had been said about Geronimo.

They had gotten their inspiration from the statue next door. The more the patrolman heard the more it sounded like something he'd probably be reading in the papers soon. *Father-Son Duo Do In Dope Fiend.* He felt broadened by the event's import.

"That part about Geronimo's good," he told Hugo. And because everything seemed to be winding up so neatly, what with crime having been foiled, he thought he'd just clear up a question he'd had in mind a long time concerning the statue next door.

"You reckon it really is him?"

Hugo and Weldon were stumped. Like the patrolman, though, they were liberated by the exhilaration of having faced Danger but averted Catastrophe, and thus were willing, given the special nature of the day, to reexamine life from new perspectives.

"You know, I don't know," Hugo explained finally. Mouth agape, Weldon gawked at the statue standing a few yards away in the center of the lot. Then they all three walked thoughtfully toward it as though to check its features against some mental image of Geronimo, though none of them had ever seen his picture.

"*You* go to school," Hugo said to Weldon, delegating authority.

"Sure looks like him," Weldon claimed. He meant that the statue had an Indian's face, and since Weldon only knew the names of two Indians, it had to be one or the other.

"Or Cochise," he added after a moment.

"That's what I was thinking," Hugo agreed.

"Huh!" the patrolman said.

They stared at the statue. Constructed in two molds, it showed an obvious seam dividing the front half from the back. Because the base wasn't large enough and because it had been set in sand, it leaned a little to the north, toward Hugo's place. Over the years, vandals had painted moustaches on its upper lip and Frankenstein scars across its forehead, and members of successive senior classes had adorned various parts of its anatomy with their totem-year, the most prominent being the aforementioned "Srs. 78" slashed across its belly by the members of Oil City's most promising graduating class in this one-stoplight hamlet.

Hugo hadn't been up close to the statue in three years, not since he had chased a softball into the pasture on a Fourth of July. He felt as if he hadn't appreciated it like he should.

"Them goddamn kids!" he growled. "Painting it up like that!"

"How do you reckon it come to be here?" the patrolman asked.

"Lots of folks ast that."

"How come, you reckon?"

"I reckon because they want to know," Hugo replied.

"No, how come it to be here?" the patrolman insisted.

Hugo sucked air through his tooth-valve. "I don't know," he admitted resentfully.

The patrolman turned to peer off toward the sheriff's car, where Gubberman sat answering questions, getting higher and higher, feeling his pulse flail the walls of his blood vessels, wanting to pour out his soul to the sheriff, tell him where things were really at, tell him how he understood perfectly that the sheriff was just doing his job and that he loved the sheriff like a brother in spite of it, that they were all in this together, all passengers on a big round rocketship hurtling quietly and marvelously through space and they had to stick together, try to love one another, that they were all just brothers passing through. A fellow-feeling for all creation billowed in his breast as the patrolman turned and yelled back to the sheriff, "Clyde? You know how this thing come to be here?"

The sheriff nodded slowly to indicate he hadn't the foggiest notion, so Gubberman leaned forward and, spurred on by his fellow feeling for the patrolman, yelled out the sheriff's window that the statue was a symbol of displaced persons everywhere. The sheriff put handcuffs on him.

Weldon kept glaring suspiciously toward the sheriff's car. The thought that maybe the statue wasn't *supposed* to be there swooped out of the inky sky like a bat, but he brained it with the broom of common sense. He spat on the ground.

"Been here far as *I* can remember," he snorted.

Western
History

One August dawn earlier in this century — when corruption was rife and our lives were not free from crime — the body of an Indian was discovered a few miles from the hamlet of Wekoka, Oklahoma. A farmer hauling water to his penned-up livestock spotted the corpse, sprawled limbs askew, in the bottom of a weedy culvert. After slipping on his spectacles, he saw that the dead man clutched a Colt pistol in his right hand. Beside him was an empty whiskey bottle.

The farmer, recent to these parts, had never seen the Indian before. The dead man was hatless, and blood from the hole in his temple had crusted on the collar of his dusty suit coat. The brogans on the dead man's feet looked new, and the farmer, a sharecropper with four children, thought sourly that somebody would probably come along and help themselves to the boots and pistol before the corpse was known to the authorities. The beneficiary might be a worthless whore or roughneck; worse, it could be another oil-rich Creek or Osage who'd been favored by riches through no effort or merit of his own, and, like this dead one, could already afford new boots, a pistol, and a bottle to hog to himself.

Most likely the Indian had drunk himself crazy then put a bullet through his skull, the farmer concluded. He shot a quick look up and down the stretch of hard-packed, washboard sand for traffic, then jumped from the wagon and limp-gaited down the avalanching sides of the culvert. Kneeling beside the Indian, he unknotted the cold stiff fingers from the pistol and crammed it into his waistband, tried unsuccessfully to wrench off the shoes but, panicky, wound up wrestling with the corpse. Finally, he forced himself to calm down and untie the laces. He left the dead man lying on his side.

He shoved the pistol and the boots beneath loose hay in the wagon bed, then shouted his mule away from the scene of the crime.

On his return an hour later, he was startled to see that the body now lay supine. Flies were swarming about the head wound in the sunlight. He guessed that the body had fallen over from where it had been reclining on a flank. This new posture suggested life in the body, as if the corpse wanted to show it was capable of haunting him.

When he led Deputy Gibbons back to the spot an hour later, he didn't mention taking the shoes and the pistol. The deputy, a thin, middle-aged bachelor with long teeth the color of Swiss cheese, stood on the running board of the county-owned Model A to look into the culvert. He stared for a time at the corpse before speaking.

"Old Henry have any money on him?" he asked the farmer suddenly.

"Damn if I know," the farmer shot back, cursing himself for not having checked.

Deputy Gibbons had once jailed Henry Roan Horse for public drunkenness. This offense was usually not uncommon or grievous enough to require arrest, but W.O. Kale had pressured the deputy to lock up the Indian because Henry had unwisely chosen to use the colored heads of the zinnias growing along the front porch of the Kale home for target practice. He hadn't harmed Mrs. Kale's zinnias, but he'd put several holes in the siding; one slug had wormed through the wall, spun up to the ceiling, then, spent, had dropped onto the table beside Julia Kale's soup bowl. Kale's daughter had fainted.

While serving time, Henry Roan Horse demonstrated that he was a worthy checkers adversary whose lapses in concentration had allowed the deputy to win three out of every five games and thus part the Creek from a few pennies each evening. He wasn't much for talk, but he did say he'd outlived two wives and most of his children. "All good folk," he told Deputy Gibbons. "I got good luck." He'd given the deputy his corn-cob pipe when his sister had bailed him out.

That had happened right before oil was struck on Henry's allottment. Since then, the countryside had been invaded by boomer trash who kept the cells full day and night, and these days the sheriff usually had to attach leg irons to an arrested prisoner and loop them around a chain that stretched between two Spanish oaks outside the jail. On any day a dozen open-air prisoners were strung along the chain like cheap charms on a gaudy bracelet. Incarcerating them in the open, the deputy couldn't prevent their drinking and playing cards with other trash who wandered by or sending children over to Jack's Cafe for steaks or even treating themselves to women after dark. The deputy had to shut his eyes to everything except someone slipping a prisoner a hacksaw or a weapon. He tried not to let it bother him; still, though, it made a small hard fist in his gut that so few people were concerned about such lawlessness.

The deputy finally stepped down into the ditch. He breathed through his mouth while searching Henry's pockets. He found a package of readymades, a folding knife that Deputy Gibbons recalled Henry had used to carve a cage-and-ball puzzle while in jail, a buffalo nickel, jelly beans with lint stuck to them, two buckeyes, a half plug of chewing tobacco, and a few bones that Deputy Gibbons knew to have come from a hawk.

"Looks like robbery to me. Henry must have got hisself hijacked," Deputy Gibbons said after he had climbed up onto the road. "You see a chestnut gelding around? I think he bought a saddle with silver trim too, not long ago."

"Didn't see no horse," said the farmer with irritation. "You figure a rich Indian'd have hisself a fancy new automobile. Or maybe bought a grand pianner and put uh engine in it."

"Henry wasn't much for machinery," said Deputy Gibbons, ignoring the farmer's sarcasm. His own comment had an eulogistic air, so the deputy let silence frame it for a moment before continuing to think aloud. "Like as not the hijacker took his mount along with his boots and whatever pocket money he had."

"Looks like they drunk his whiskey, too."

"Naw. That bottle's been there a long time. Old Henry went Baptist a while back." It was shortly after his last arrest, as a matter of fact, but Deputy Gibbons kept the information to himself.

Dismissed, the farmer wished the deputy luck in finding the hijackers then drove off in his wagon eager to search for the chestnut gelding with a silver-trimmed saddle that had wandered away after the Indian had killed himself.

To Deputy Gibbons fell the unhappy task of taking Henry Roan Horse's body to his sister, Mollie Buhalter. He drove back into town to exchange the Model A for his own wagon, then loaded the corpse onto the bed of planks. That Henry's feet were bare outraged him.

To reach the Buhalters', he had to take a road that cut through a section of drilling rigs. Several times on the way he pulled the wagon to the shoulder and had to soft-talk the jittery horse while an oily truck thundered past. With Henry's corpse covered by a blanket on the floor, he felt like the driver of a one-wagon cortege; that he had to veer off the road for traffic added insult to injury.

Here the fields were the color of a cockroach; the trees and bushes were drenched and shining with crude oil. The midday summer sun kneaded the fumes until the chemical stench made the deputy almost swoon. Machinery clanked and hissed as they passed the rigs. A month ago, south of town, a gusher had sent oil pouring into Little Bow Creek; it caught fire and boiled for a week, killing everything in the water and burning down the trees that lined the stream. Water that burned, air you couldn't breathe — these oil men had created a Hell on Earth here. Its denizens surrounded him on the road: trucks, wagons, autos, men carrying pipes or pushing carts and barrows, children shouldering wooden yokes heavy with dangling buckets of water meant for their families, who lived in tents.

Though most people in town knew Henry Roan Horse, few of these transients would. But any stranger encountering him could've guessed he was rich. The Spanish saddle was such as a wealthy white man might ride in a rodeo parade and had little use other than to let people know its owner had money. Coming along this road, Henry could've easily caught the eye of a desperado who'd shoot him for the horse and saddle and boots with the indifference of swatting a gnat.

The deputy delivered Henry's body to the home of his sister and brother-in-law and consoled them as best he could. He assured them he'd find the killer, though privately he doubted he'd ever learn more.

Unaware that the bereaved were about to join Henry in the hereafter — they and their cabin would soon be dynamited into smithereens by a hopeful beneficiary — Deputy Gibbons went to eat a late lunch at Jack's Cafe. The cafe was crammed with noisy oil men; he was jostled when he raised his fork, so by the time he'd shoveled down his stew, he'd stabbed himself in his cheek and his chin.

He left the cafe in a bad mood. He decided that when he got to the jail he'd brew himself a decent cup of coffee and, if necessary, lock himself in the outhouse to enjoy it in peace and quiet.

The sheriff spoiled his plan by being in when the deputy returned, and that was unusual. The sheriff had a lot of land to look after, and he appeared to own more each year. The deputy often wondered why the sheriff had bothered to run for reelection because he rarely expressed interest in maintaining law and order in the county. The deputy suspected the sheriff's motive for staying in office was connected to the miraculously growing acreage, but he didn't know how, and he couldn't investigate because he was far too busy clearing the streets of corpses.

Deputy Gibbons brewed the promised coffee but had to do the sheriff's paper work while he drank it. He could hear the sheriff's scratchy voice echo down the hallway as he talked to a whore they'd locked up in the jail's only closet due to press of space. The sheriff was a windbag; his favored recreation was to lean against the cell bars and reminisce with a prisoner about his own outlaw youth. He also enjoyed feinting bargains with the prisoners for their freedom (at least, the deputy presumed the sheriff was only feinting).

The whore had been confined to the closet for a week on a charge of killing a drunk geologist who had beaten her severely before she'd gone for a gun. The sheriff was saying he would let her out of jail if she would come be his maid while she was awaiting trial. Deputy Gibbons had a hard time picturing the sheriff engaged in sexual intercourse, though it wasn't so hard to imagine him standing with his trousers slopped about his ankles. The sheriff reminded the deputy of a frog. He was a frog-faced man with froggy arms and stubby, froggy fingers; he spoke in a froggy voice, thought frog thoughts like a stew made from pond mud squeezed through a sieve.

When the sheriff went outside to the porch to enjoy a larger audience, Deputy Gibbons went back to the open closet where the whore sat crosslegged on the floor with her face dropped into one palm. Her girlfriends had decorated the cast on her right arm with colored ribbons.

"What did you tell him?"

"Who?" She raised her head. One cheek was still swollen and purple.

"Sheriff Miller."

"I didn't tell him nothing!" she hissed.

"Naw, I meant about being his maid."

The girl eyed the deputy with suspicion. "I told him I'd as soon hang from a rope as let him lie on me."

To her surprise, the deputy laughed.

That night, while Deputy Gibbons lay fidgeting in bed, he imagined that the sheriff and some leading men in town such as W.O. Kale who had the deputy at their beck and call were engaged in a conspiracy to get as rich as they could as fast as they could, at everyone else's expense and without any consideration for the law. He hated to be so cynical and pessimistic. He tried to deny his suspicions, arguing that they were provoked by the proximity of so many gamblers, extortionists, hijackers, and hoodwinkers. He told himself such suspicions were just another sign of how the poison that had flooded his quiet hamlet had seeped into his skull.

He thought of how he had had to arrest Henry, and why. He recalled taking those few pennies in checkers and felt bad about them, believing now that Henry had lost those games to pique the deputy's interest and to pay for the companionship. Like a lot of Indians, he was the soul of hospitality, even if only in his jail cell.

If Deputy Gibbons hadn't played checkers with Henry, then it wouldn't have mattered so much that he got hijacked, and he'd be just another corpse. Since the boom began, the deputy had thought he'd grown used to dragging corpses out of ditches, boardinghouses, tents, or shallow graves, corpses of Indians, white men, Negroes, roughnecks, gamblers who won too much too fast, confidence men whose tongues were nimble but whose feet were not, whores who ran off with good men, and former partners in mushrooming businesses.

Henry Roan Horse had ended up among them, to the deputy's sorrow. The deputy was too monkish, watchful, and reserved to be intimate with most people, but he felt closer to Henry than to most of those whose corpses he had transported from their point of abandonment to whoever would receive them for whatever reason.

He remembered the whore saying she'd rather hang from a rope than let the sheriff lie on her.

The next morning he decided to interview the farmer and take him back to the ditch to make sure no clue had been overlooked. He struck out for the farmer's cabin in his wagon, since the sheriff had commandeered the Model A for his personal use. Gibbons recalled the pang of irritation on the farmer's face when he had mentioned the horse and saddle. It could have been an expression of indignation at being accused, however indirectly, of having taken them. Deputy Gibbons didn't believe the farmer had seen the animal or taken it himself, but he could tell the farmer regretted having done his civic duty. The rewards for virtue were practically as nonexistent as the punishment for crime. Justice was served, if at all, by the victim's kin, and Henry's killer would have little to fear — Henry's relatives numbered Mollie, her husband, and whatever white lawyer had talked the Bureau of Indian Affairs into declaring him their financial guardian.

He found the farmer's cabin without trouble. It was within sight of the road, and no sooner had he halted the horse and looked over a field of withered corn than he spotted Henry's horse calmly crunching hay inside a worm-fenced corral. It was possible the farmer had found the animal after their conversation and was waiting for the deputy's return to release it, of course; it was also possible the farmer had found it after the conversation and planned to keep it, as well as possible the farmer had shot Henry to get it.

He could hear a child's voice yelling but couldn't make out the words. Smoke rose behind the cabin from a wash fire, he guessed. The deputy recalled that the roof of this cabin had once burned. He guessed that when the farmer moved in to sharecrop this land owned by a prosperous Creek, he had fashioned the present makeshift roof of browning boughs, like that of a brush arbor. It wouldn't keep out fall rains or winter cold. Why hadn't the farmer fixed the roof permanently?

He geed his horse back into a walk and headed the wagon down the road beyond the cabin, following the border of a vegetable patch whose greenery displayed a patina of ruddy dust. A few visible melons were cracking from the heat and drought.

The farmer was mending a fence a half mile from the cabin, hardly a stone's throw from the road. He looked up as the wagon approached. He had a coil of barbed-wire held in one hand and a hammer in the other.

When the deputy stopped the wagon, the farmer was frozen like a scarecrow, fencing staples pinched between his lips. He squinted at the deputy.

"Ooo izz it?"

"Deputy Gibbons."

The farmer spat out the staples into his hand, cocked his hat brim back with his forearm and swabbed at his forehead with his sleeve.

"Find out who hijacked that Indian?"

The farmer was shod in a pair of new brogans. Henry's bare toes rose to the deputy's mind. He found it hard to believe the farmer was so stupid.

"I think so." In the silence, the deputy felt his gorge rising. "You see that horse and saddle I mentioned yesterday?"

The farmer looked down the road and then into the hills as if to make one last scan for the horse before giving up, then shook his head slowly. The deputy watched with exasperation, feeling insulted.

"Where'd you get them new boots?"

"Bought 'em in town."

"How about that chestnut gelding in the corral by your house. You buy that, too?"

"Yep."

"Got a bill of sale?"

The farmer licked his lips and glanced about as if for an escape route.

"Lost it."

"Shit! You take me for a goddman idiot?" The deputy squelched an impulse to jump down and beat the farmer to within an inch of his life. The farmer looked nervous and bewildered, as if puzzled as to how the death of a drunken, aging Indian could become so important.

"If you think I killed that Indian then robbed him, then how come I showed you where he was? If I'd a thought I was going to get myself in a lot of hot water by doing the right thing, then I'll be go-to-Hell if I'd a done it!"

Deputy Gibbons rolled his eyes. "Get in the wagon." He tossed the reins over the footboard and climbed into the bed. The planks showed a rusty stain where Henry's body had lain. The farmer hesitated, then he laid down the coil of wire, kicked loose grass over it, threaded himself gingerly through the strands of barbs, and, carrying the hammer, walked to the wagon.

"Leave the hammer here."

"I'm gonna give it to yew, I sure as Hell don't wanna leave it here so some Injun'll steal it."

Deputy Gibbons took the hammer, suppressing an urge to bash in the farmer's skull.

When the farmer had climbed up into the seat, Deputy Gibbons said, "Pick up the reins and drive back to town."

"How come?" The farmer craned his neck, his eyes bulging as he looked at the deputy.

Deputy Gibbons dug a plug of tobacco out of his shirt pocket, took a bite, then merely glared at the farmer. Let him think the worst — it might pry out some truth.

The farmer clucked the horse into motion. The deputy

stared at the line dividing the farmer's raw sunburnt nape from the collar. The farmer's hair was dusty; the hat was dusty; the farmer's neck was dusty, and sweat made little channels in it. The collar of his gray twill shirt was frayed and soiled along the crease. His shoulders seemed to twitch as the wagon bumped along, and the deputy knew the silence was getting to the farmer, and that pleased him. The farmer had a lot to think about. The deputy didn't know for sure what the farmer was guilty of, but plainly the farmer was guilty, if only of being born. The shoulder seams of the man's gray shirt dropped below the rounded humps at the top of his arms; the farmer was a scrawny, nervous sort with freckles and water-stained teeth. His feet would twitch in a little dance when the noose popped his neck.

Possibly he bullied his wife, his children, and his animals but would always grovel before other men and back-clap them. He lacked the spunk for a life of crime, the deputy could see that. He was just your ordinary weak moronic human being whose ire had been aroused by the sight of Henry Roan Horse coming along this road too many mornings, and he had decided that it was more right for a white man to wear those boots and to ride that horse and have the saddle (hidden now, to be sold later most likely) than for a red savage to possess them. The farmer had taken his envy and made a virtue of it, the deputy guessed.

Deputy Gibbons stared at the farmer's back, imagining how the bullet might snap the man's candy-cane spine, then explode out of his chest like a flushed quail.

"What'd you do with the saddle?"

"What saddle?"

"What saddle you think?"

"I swear to God I didn't do nothing to that Indian."

The deputy drew out his pistol, cocked it, and aimed it

at the farmer's back. The metallic ratcheting was unmis-
takeable to the farmer's ears.

"I swear I didn't!"

"His boots just walk by and gobble up your feet? That
horse just break down the gate to your corral to get himself
locked up in it as quick as he could?"

"I found the horse last night. I never knowed he even
had one until you said so, I swear. I was going to turn him
in."

The lie was so pathetic it made the deputy speechless
with melancholy. Did the farmer forget he had just claimed
to have bought the horse?

The farmer took the silence as an opportunity to press
his case and said, more calmly, "Besides, what're you getting so riled up for? Maybe he prolly killed hisself and
somebody took his pistol. You got no proof anybody killed
him, do you? At least not any that'd hold up in court. I'm
not saying I did it or nothing. I just don't understand why
you take it personal."

"Because you're a lying sonofabitch. And I'm tired of
looking at lying sonsabitches and locking them up and listening to them lie. I'm tired of dragging their corpses
around because they lied once too often to some other
lying sonofabitch."

"Hey, now!" the farmer said, puffing up indignantly,
"Wait just a — "

"And you're one lying sonofabitch that's not going to
get away with it. I'm going to lock you up, and I'm going
to see to it that they hang your sorry ass."

Deputy Gibbons paused momentarily to study the twitch
in the man's shoulders. The farmer was winding himself
tighter and tighter, the deputy could see that, and so he rel-
ished tightening the screw.

"Maybe your old lady and your children can get along

without you, maybe they can't. I don't care myself. I seen your old lady. Maybe she'll tell me where those boots and that horse come from. I got ways of making people tell me things."

"I didn't kill that Indian. I swear I didn't. I just come along and there he was lyin' in the ditch! My old lady and kids they don't know nothing about this."

"Where's that silver saddle?"

"There wasn't no saddle!" the farmer screeched.

"Well," said the deputy calmly, "you best kiss your freedom goodby, my friend. You're gonna get locked away for a long time."

Deputy Gibbons belabored the point because he knew that what the farmer had intimated earlier was true, unfortunately: no jury would convict this white farmer for killing that Indian, especially with no proof but a pair of new boots and a horse that had walked itself into his corral. That's why I take it so personal, he thought — because nobody else does.

The deputy watched the twitch grow more pronounced as the wagon rolled on, yard after yard. Still two or three miles from town, they were approaching the spot where the farmer had claimed he had found Henry Roan Horse in the bar ditch. The farmer bounced an inch or so higher with every rut that jolted the wheels; his toes tapped the wagon bed; his shoulders hunched, dropped forward as if he were about to propel himself off a cliff or take flight; his ear waggled as he worked his jaw muscles. He was coiling himself tighter and tighter, dropping one hand onto the side and holding the reins in the other.

The deputy waited, silent, slowly working his chaw between his molars, watching the farmer's body jerk from some inward spasm like a gut cramp. The deputy figured the farmer would soon jump out of the wagon.

Silently, he raised the pistol and pointed it at the farmer's back, aligning the sight along the man's spine about a foot below his neck.

The farmer's left palm was flattened on the wagon's top rail, the back of it white from pressing it down. His feet were arched, his Achilles tendons stiff. He seemed to be gathering his breath, rising slightly, perhaps counting to himself.

Ahead was the culvert where the deputy had picked up the body of his Creek friend the farmer had killed and robbed. The farmer raised the hand holding the reins, and it looked to the deputy as if he were about to snap the reins to make the horse run.

Deputy Gibbons tightened his trigger finger. The farmer's back swelled as he took a deep breath, his right hand went up, came down, then his body rose off the wagon seat, his left hand mushroomed against the rail as he appeared to push himself off, but he had risen only about two inches — as far as he might bounce from the wagon's hitting a chuckhole — when the deputy was startled by a loud pop and an unseen force slamming into the farmer's back. The farmer went somersaulting off the seat; he flew through the air upside down and away from the wagon, his ruddy, gouged-out chest visible to the deputy for an instant, and then he fell to the shoulder and rolled down the side of the ditch.

The horse whinnied and broke into a gallop. The deputy scrambled into the seat, retrieved the reins and tugged the wide-eyed horse to a stop. Deputy Gibbons was panting. He couldn't recall having pulled the trigger; he couldn't recall even willing it pulled. Belatedly, he looked up and down the road, but no one was coming. He climbed down off the wagon then trotted the several yards to where the farmer lay face down in the culvert.

Staring at the farmer's neck, the deputy stood on the road for a long time, thinking that there was no one to ask anything of now. Suspect shot while trying to escape. For once the deputy wouldn't have to endure the maddening certainty that a crime would go unpunished. Henry Roan Horse played a good game of checkers; he minded his own business. When poor, he coveted nothing.

The Man
With
Unusual
Luck

*E*ven now six months later Arturo Sánchez's death puzzles us as much as his arrival eleven years ago, when he appeared clad in dusty rags we later learned he had torn to shreds himself. He took a hut at the edge of the village and went to work in the silver mines. He hardly spoke, though now and then he poked his handsome, sour face out of his doorway to tongue-lash the children for dragging sticks in the dirt beneath his window.

"He appears old only because he doesn't wash the grime off his face after work," the neighbors said. "And that's because he has no woman." Maiden aunts were sent in pairs with sugar candies, but if Arturo Sánchez ever saw one thing leading to another, no one knew. One reported that he endured the calls the way a man kneeling at communion longs to rise from aching knees.

Some say he lived like a monk. Others that he only tried. No one saw him take a woman to his hut, at least, and those who claimed that he visited the *putas* in Irapuato always added that while most men went off in high spirits and returned in shame, our Señor Sánchez trudged away long-faced and came trodding home the same.

So he lived ten yars among us known to none until a blast from leaking gas in the mine flung a beam against his legs, snapping them like straws. The rescuers lugged him and four corpses of his fellow workers back to the village, where he writhed in agony on his *petate* as Dr. Hernández cut away his flesh to set the jagged hunks of bone back into his thigh. He refused to take a bed in the Guanajuato hospital, and so he came to know Belén, Hernández's maid, who helped make the casts for his legs and who, on the doctor's instructions, salved the man's eyes and bandaged them.

"Will I be blind forever?"

"Not if you're lucky, *hombre*," the doctor said.

Sánchez scoffed despite his pain.

"But you survived!" argued Dr. Hernández. "I'd call that luck!"

"It depends on what follows."

"A pessimist, eh?"

"A realist. What God made me."

The waiting room of the doctor's office in Guanajuato was far too crowded to allow him to come to the hut but once in a while, so he rented the services of his maid to Sánchez. The crones began to cackle — was a match in this? Belén's husband had left three years ago to work on a highway in Guatamela, where he died of malaria. They had heard her pray to be forgiven for running him off. The crones counted her assets: she was good-hearted; she had lively black eyes set in a broad face still untouched by her troubles. Her body was young and strong even after four children.

But they bat about her liabilities, too: she could not seem to avoid accidents that turned an ankle or burned an arm or cut a finger; she was impetuous; she was haughty because her sister was a teacher, and she was prone to melancholy. Too, some hinted that she had no need of a husband.

But Belén was playing hard to get! She complained to the doctor for extending her duties, then bustled into Sánchez's hut, set a pot of beans on the table, filled the water glass beside his pallet, applied the salve and bandages without a word, then rushed away to finish her chores at the doctor's house. Sánchez's neighbor claimed she was in and out in five minutes.

Belén herself told of how the next day the man did not appear to have stirred. The glass was empty, but the beans had dried in the pot. Annoyed by this waste, she uttered her first words to him.

"You had no hunger?"

"Yes."

"Then why didn't you eat the beans, man?" she snapped.

"What beans?"

She blushed almost purple. Even had he seen the pot, he could not have reached it! "Ah! *Me lo siento*! How stupid of me!" She must have wondered, was this the neglect which drove her husband off? She bathed him, changed his clothes, dumped his slop jar. Naturally they talked, and soon she was soliciting from us little gifts of cigarettes and candy. Her powers of persuasion on behalf of his comfort were amazing: from Espinosa the grocer she got a bed, arguing that a man with broken legs needed more than a pallet of straw over dirt. You can be sure that tongues flapped then, and the gossips wondered aloud if she was too proud to lie on the floor! More charitable souls talked about a wedding — his eyes would heal and there Belén would be before him — prettier than a picture. What a fine, romantic story it would make!

"Yes, yes, how fortunate you are," Dr. Hernández murmured as he peeled away the bandages. He soaked Sánchez's eyes in a medicinal solution and patted them dry with a towel. Belén stood quietly in the dimness along the wall of the hut.

Sánchez slowly raised his eyelids. He gazed at the doctor in silence. Then, at last, his dark pupils flicked away to search out the woman's face. When their eyes met, he shuddered.

"Go to the Devil!" he snarled, his cheeks twitching like landed fish.

Biting her lip, Belén ran from the room. Later to us she showed a face stony with indifference, but we could imagine her humiliation — a woman whose family included teachers and homeowners had sought the attentions of a man most thought hardly better than a beggar, only to be cursed and cast aside! Some claimed that God was punishing her for neglecting her husband and for shunning the advances of other, more worthy villagers. (And for the secret lover which would account for both!)

"My blindness trapped me, tied me to her in ways I had not known," Sánchez sighed with exhaustion as he talked to our young priest, Father Montejano, who had decided the situation required his attention. "I could hear her skirt brushing the edge of the bed she brought me, I could feel it against my arm, and I could hear her breath coming hard as she grunted to lift things. *Por Dios!* If it had been but that. . . ."

"And what else?"

"Her smell."

Father Montejano's ears perked up.

"She smelled of soap and bread, sometimes of sweat. Once of her curse."

"It is a hard thing to live alone," said our young Father.

"I could feel her fingers on my face when she changed my bandages and I tried to picture her body. When we talked I tried to see the face in her voice. And because she reminded me of the family I once had I wanted her to be ugly, you understand?"

"Only if the memories are unpleasant."

Sánchez pressed the gauze into his eyes with his palms. "There is no word for it," he muttered.

"Were you unlucky in love?"

"Yes."

"It might not be that way again."

Arturo Sánchez then talked about his past. Although he was only a *campesino*, he had taught himself to read and write and had always wanted to study law or philosophy. And this — the life of a teacher or a lawyer or a landowner — he desired this for his son, not the life of a peasant. So he forced the boy to attend school even when he would have been useful in the *milpas* planting or harvesting. To amuse him and to encourage quickness of mind, he taught his son card tricks he had learned in the *pulquerias*.

But by sixteen the boy proved lazy as a stone and just as ambitious. They shouted at each other sunup to sundown until in exasperation Sánchez banished his son from his home. The boy made his way to the great capital, then to Morélia to Guadalajara and back in an ever-quickening circle, playing the shell game in villages along the way and taking money from the suckers. One year later word returned that against sound advice he had gone into a village where an epidemic had fired a gambling fever to a white-hot pitch and he had in only a few hours won a small fortune before contracting scarlet fever.

"You must not blame yourself. Sons leave their homes whether they are sent away or not. But I can see you are not reassured."

"He was unlucky. He got his crooked fate from me."

"He was also stupid." Father Montejano hoped the brutality would shock Sánchez out of his melancholy. "Maybe even greedy. And for that you are not altogether to blame. It's arrogant of you to presume so much control over another's life, even if that life came from your loins."

"Only one without children could say so, Father," Sánchez said sourly.

But the next day he apologized to Belén in a faltering voice for his peculiar outburst. Humbly, he asked her to serve him while his legs healed and offered to repay her double when he was up again. (Understandably, she hesitated before agreeing.) When Father Montejano brought Belén's eldest son, Carlos, to his hut to play checkers, though, Sánchez looked up into the priest's face like an animal seeing the door to a trap close behind him.

"A childless father and a fatherless child," Father Montejano mumbled apologetically to the bewildered man after the boy had gone.

"But the woman. . . ."

"It won't kill you to love her. In spite of her fear and whatever mystery makes her curse herself, she has much love for you. She has had her trials too, you know!"

"Yes. But I may bring her still another. My luck — "

"That's nonsense!" the priest cut in gruffly. "Quit talking like an Indian. If there's no other way, think of the woman's love as penance for your own despair."

He did so, but with great reluctance. Belén and her son

came daily to keep his house. In their company he was
either mute or garrulous. It was as though, some said, the
woman and boy were a temptation to be resisted but to
which he often succumbed. Sometimes, inexplicably, he
waved them out of his hut with irritation. Meanwhile, the
gossips waited for his legs to heal enough to have his casts
removed, when Belén would have no more excuse for
going to him (and neglecting her own family and shirking
her duties at the doctor's house). Though for some time he
had been up on crutches, he never ventured outside of his
hut — perhaps if he had seemed too able, she would have
felt foolish.

Sánchez asked about a job. One of the shafts had flooded after the explosion and only half the miners could return
to the mine. Those left unemployed had taken other jobs in
the village. Work was scarce, but Dr. Hernández got a good
buy in a herd of goats, and his former gardener overheard
Belén argue to the doctor that he would need a *chivadór*.
After all, he was hardly a tender of goats himself, so would
he hire Sánchez?

"As a favor to you, *querida*?" the doctor asked.

"Si."

A livelihood secured, all yearned for the proposal and the
wedding.

He did not come to her on the first day after the casts
were removed, when he limped about the village on a cane
her son had carved from mesquite. She had stayed home,
too proud to go to his hut. He did not appear on the second day, either, when he began work as the doctor's
chivadór. On the third he hobbled by her house but did
not hail her. By the next day his ingratitude had aroused
the fury of many villagers. How dare this stranger (this,
even after a decade!) take advantage of her!

On the fifth day, just after Sánchez had pulled off his

dusty clothes and was stepping into a washtub filled with water, a clamor arose at his door like a club knocked madly against it, and as he stood naked, his arm still arching out to drape his trousers over the post of a chair, her son lunged into the room and looked wildly about, his jaw wagging.

"My mother got that bed for you!" he blurted out at last in tears, then dashed out the door.

They sat with the tub of unused water between them, the priest has said, and as they talked the man ran his glance in and out of the doorway to the street like the pendulum of a clock.

"Father, for twelve years I have wanted another family."

"It is within reach."

"No. I am no longer young, and my luck is too poor — "

Father Montejano tried to stifle his annoyance. "*Mira*, my son, this thing about your luck is tiresome. Your pity for yourself is unmanly."

"But you don't know — " Sánchez then broke off and swung his gaze into the priest's eyes. "I killed my daughter."

Shocked, Father Montejano kept silent, afraid to intrude as the man's head dropped forward over the tub; his shoulders jerked and the surface of the water broke into rings of concentric ripples.

"After my son's death, I went crazy," he continued after he had calmed himself. "I would wake up in my *milpa* of the *ejido* with my hoe in my hand, chopping madly at the cornstalks while I screamed blasphemies at the top of my lungs. My neighbors would watch with fear and amazement, but they were no more surprised than I.

"I got drunk often. I was a sorry sight, I guess. My daughter was living in Dolores Hidalgo with her new husband, a butcher. Since I had had no wife for many years, my daughter had cared for us like a mother, but with my son dead, when I drank I could not contain — " He paused to lay his hands upon the sides of a giant, invisible ball in the air, " — my emptiness. I called her. 'Come see your poor Papa,' I pleaded. 'You're all I have left in this world!' It was late in the evening. '*En la manana*, Papa,' she said. But I painted vivid pictures of my grief, accused her of neglect, cursed her and ordered her to come that very night." Sánchez clenched his teeth, then turned his face into the shadows. "She came. And the bus went through a guard rail in the mountains. The driver was drunk."

Father Montejano wanted to shout with relief, but he managed to murmur his sympathy for the loss.

"She was yet childless," Sánchez added.

"And you feel responsible."

"Father, I don't want this to happen again, for *my* sake! My son and daughter were lucky; they were not left to grieve!"

"That is a weak-spirited way to look at life," chided the Father. "Be a man."

"Father, save that for the boys. You want me to accept my suffering in silence, but since I never asked God to make a Job of me, I will not accept the task. To accuse me of self-pity and weakness, you must match your good fortune with my ill luck."

"Leave the theology to me," Father Montejano replied. "A man your age should have learned to accept what comes without a lot of belly-aching. You should consider yourself lucky to have been saved from death and to have a chance for a second family. Not everyone is so blessed."

Sánchez smiled wryly. "Some are more fortunate than others. As for the accident in the mines, that was not my first escape. But — " he sighed, "you are right. He who is afraid to live is already dead, and I have great fear of loneliness.

"But I have learned this, too, Father — " He looked sternly at the priest. "God has designs on me which would appall you to look at without flinching. He has been using me as an example — "

"*Hombre*! There's nothing but human stupidity and greed and indulgence to explain your bad luck, as you call it!" Father Montejano slapped at his thigh with barely contained agitation. "Quit whining and take advantage of the blessings that come your way. The woman and her children can resurrect you from this grave of despondency, believe me!"

Most of us would say Sánchez had longed to be convinced; at least he lost no time the next morning tramping to Belén's house in clean *calzones* and a white shirt. He smiled wanly at the children and dogs that scurried behind him as he hobbled toward his future *nóvia*.

But when he stepped from her house minutes later, his face was long, and he locked his eyes onto the street before him.

Was she being coy? Or was she out to get revenge — a suitor should yearn, not slink in to propose like a whipped dog! But, everyone whispered, she better be careful not to make an obstacle too great to overcome.

"Don't let this discourage you," Father Montejano counseled. "Perhaps she feels unworthy of you."

Sánchez returned once more to face her "no," but on the third try, she gave in.

Before the wedding Sánchez seemed torn between celebrating his good luck and protecting it with desperation. He brought a *curandera* down from the hills to sweep the cobwebs of ill luck from the corners of Belén's rooms. Passersby heard the old woman groaning and chanting while some vile concoction steamed on the stove. Although

Belén submitted to the intrusion with good cheer, the priest was furious.

"You're acting like an old woman!" he told Sánchez. "Don't tempt God's anger by denying his bounty — if you fear the future, pray!"

Everyone saw that Sánchez struggled to control his fear that a catastrophe would prevent the wedding. He apologized for the trouble his anxiety caused Belén and begged her understanding.

But then he would rush to her at odd moments to plead that she not leave the house because he had had a premonition. She humored him, but as the wedding drew closer, her eyes dulled like two clay marbles and her face hardened into a mask. Once she disappeared for an evening and no one could account for her absence.

"Where were you?" Sánchez demanded fearfully.

"I went to Guanajuato. To pray."

It helped, everyone said. As her sister and two helpers fit her for the wedding dress, she blushed and giggled like a girl.

"Can't you quit twitching and pull that gut in?" her sister teased with a lewd wink at the helpers.

"Like a burro plays a flute!" one of the helpers sniggered.

"Ah, *mamacita*!" Her sister poked at her belly. "You're not the girl you used to be — you think the old man likes a little padding?"

"We'll seam it loose in case he's in a hurry!" the other helper joked. Belén wailed with laughter, her face flushed as with a fever.

On that most important morning the groom wrung his hands and moaned that all would not go well. But in vain — Arturo Sánchez was meant to have the happiness of a second wife; the wedding went uninterrupted by God or man. And at the fiesta, while the photographer tried to pose the two in solemn dignity, Sánchez's mouth kept springing open like rubber into a grin; released from his prison of superstition, he beamed at nothing like a crazy man.

"What do you think, now, eh?" Father Montejano called out merrily.

Sánchez whooped and waved his cane. "Father!" he crowed. "Most of my life I've been a fool whose only wisdom was to stay alive for this!"

But neither enjoyed his triumph very long. Whatever apparition of bliss had lured the man out of his sanctuary of isolation vanished soon after the wedding when a truck struck Belén down in the highway which cuts the village into its higher and lower halves. The driver was rushing a load of chickens to the great capital. He claimed that the woman had her face directed toward him, and for that reason he did not slow down — to his horror she dashed away from the shoulder and into the path of the truck. He felt her body thump under the wheels; he lost control and the truck careened over on its side and slid down the rain-slickened road, narrowly missing several houses and spewing a trail of broken crates and bleeding chickens down the length of the village.

The driver was knocked unconscious; the screech of brakes, the grinding slide of the truck, and the mad squawks of the chickens brought the villagers running. Gleefully, many scooped up the carcasses and ran home with the news of tomorrow's *pollo*. "It's raining chickens!" they joked. As three boys sprinted away, giggling, with their arms choked with dead and dying fowls, they tripped over Belén's body.

When Dr. Hernández arrived, Father Montejano was bent over her body, muttering. Her legs still lay in the highway because, naturally, the police had to know where the body had come to rest.

"You are much too late!" Father Montejano told the doctor acidly.

"Was there a confession?" Dr. Hernández asked with concern.

"No."

They say the priest and the doctor looked at each other for a moment as if they had a secret.

When Father Montejano went to deliver the news to the groom, he found Sánchez in a black humor, slumped in a chair as he whacked at the floor with his cane, slowly and methodically. Before Father Montejano could prepare him for the coming blow, Sánchez cursed Belén in a long violent oath which shocked the priest into frozen bewilderment.

"The whore had a lover!" Sánchez spat at last.

"Still?" blurted out Father Montejano.

"How can a man know? She has his child in her womb and wants me to rear it as my own! She was too cowardly to speak of it before now!"

"No doubt she was frightened. Did she ask to be forgiven?"

"Yes." He exhaled as though ridding himself of his anger. "I ran her off," he added morosely.

Father Montejano rose from his chair, his young frame trembling with fury. "Until now, you've had no reason to blame yourself for the grief that has come to your life. But now. . . now you must face yourself. . . and be. . .be appalled by what you see!"

He left without telling Sánchez of Belén's death. That task was left to her eldest son, who burst in upon the man much as he did during the "courtship," though this time he was not content to shout out a reproach — he tried to dash Sanchez's brains out with a shovel. Belén's sister came upon them as they were countering each other about in the room in a deadly dance, the boy huffing and choking back his sobs between clenched teeth while he swung the shovel in a wild arc that sent the blade crashing into the dishes still on the table from *comida*. Sánchez was stumbling about without his cane, trying to keep the table between them, his forehead bleeding from a large gash above his eye. "Murderer!" the boy kept blubbering.

Sánchez managed to flee the house, then disappeared. Rumors sprang up like toadstools after a rain — that he had killed her, had thrown her body beneath the truck and was hiding to avoid arrest; that he was wandering, mad with grief, in the hills; that he had gone to kill her lover. Felipe Gómez, the mortician's assistant, said that Belén's body had produced an embryo of three month's growth. Dr. Hernández had overlooked this unborn child in making his investigation prior to filling out her death certificate, but considering her closeness to him and his family, this lapse can be explained.

So many questions remained that a search party struck out the next morning into the hills but had no luck until long after noon, when the pained, insistent yapping of a dog drew their attention. They climbed to the top of the highest ridge behind the village. They found his cane lying on the ground, and beneath, at the bottom of an arroyo, crumpled atop a boulder like a rag-man, lay old Sánchez in a patch of his own brownish blood. Beside him the dog sat upright on its front legs, yowling piteously from the pain in its broken hindquarters.

Except for Father Montejano, who blushes, leaves the room or tries to change the subject, everyone enjoys discussing his own theory as to what happened. Some say he heard the injured dog whimpering and, trying to rescue it, he fell down. That, though, is not a popular theory. Others say that the dog was with him and they both fell. Most, however, think that he leaped from the ridge but was not killed at once upon impact; he cried out for help and the dog leaped after him, drawn by his voice.

"Poor Sánchez! What bad luck he had!" some say. "What? How so? He was blessed with good fortune!" others cry.

So the debate goes, endlessly it seems to those whose ears are tired and whose memories are wrapping the shroud of the past around him. We sent a death notice to his former residence, and five months later we received information from there which did nothing to settle the matter.

It seems Señor Sánchez had been an orphan. He had married an orphan. Soon there followed the two children. Then, during the persecution of the Chuch in 1926, he and his wife travelled to the capital to have his lungs checked for tuberculosis.

After a hard journey first by cart then by foot, they stopped to rest in Chapultepec Park just a few meters from where General Obregon's limousine was parked at the curb. His wife had just eased herself down on the grass with her legs crossed beneath her and her back against a pepper tree when a grenade hurled from a passing car sailed over the limousine and landed in her lap. Without a word she glanced up at Sánchez standing beside her, then doubled over and embraced the blast.

Some time later he was told his lungs were sound.

Child
Guidance

*A*fter Henry found us our house, we spent an evening inventing TV movies about him. Inspired by the mountain air and several shots of tequila, we tried to see how bad we could make it. My idea was to have a tough little urchin con an irascible American spinster out of ten dollars but teach her, inadvertently, how to love. Jack thought we should make the protagonist a cynical, down-and-out priest whose hope is restored by a child's simple act of faith, but neither of us could think of a simple act of faith.

To Henry's script we added Gutiérrez, the old *chivadór* who brought the goats down daily from the hills, following them, around twilight, through the cobblestone street below our terrace. We could make an Old Man With Young

Boy as Companion story, we said — trot out all the props for "peasant life," surround the two with earthy women and strong, slow-talking men who hunker on their heels and speak in numerous *hombres, muchos,* and *muy biens.* Later we learned the old goat-herder hobbled because one leg had been crushed in a mining accident, that he was a part-time carpenter as well, and his first name was Jesús. We were surprised at how reality mocked our burlesques of it, and an uneasiness crept into our irony about Gutiérrez, a fear, perhaps, of being mocked. Later, after we understood the real connection between Henry and the old man, the fun went out of playing with their story, and the joke, if there was one, came back to haunt us.

Henry was one of a couple dozen children who swarmed the car, yelling and jostling for position, when we stopped on the outskirts of Guanajuato to admire the purple bougainvillea plunging down walls that bordered the winding road. The car rocked as three hopped onto the rear bumper so I couldn't drive away.

I took Henry's card at random among those thrust into my window. The labored scrawl on it claimed Henry was "a very good guide."

"Okay, Enrique, hop in."

He hopped in on the passenger side, forcing Jack into the middle. "You want to see Gorki Gonzales the famous potter or you want to see the statue of Pípila or the seven plazas or the museum or — "

"Hold on," Jack cut in. "You're the guide — you tell us what we want to see."

"I just did!" Henry grinned. In the rear seat, Dorothy and Midge chuckled.

Clad in blue jeans, a faded yellow T-shirt and sandals soled with sections of tire, he perched on the seat and directed us into the subterranean passage beneath the town. To my surprise he turned out to be what his card had claimed — as we approached the mouth of the tunnel where three ramps converged, Henry tensed. "Watch it! Sometimes people — " and just as I braked, an old school bus plunged into my lane from an adjacent access, the driver ignoring traffic.

A film of dry, reddish dust coated the tops of his feet, his clothing, his arms and face, his hair; when he bounced on the seat aureoles rushed up into the sunlight. As he chattered, his long black hair flicked across his forehead, and he grinned at Dorothy and Midge in a cocky, insolent way that delighted them but gave me the impression that had we not hired him he might've deflated our tires.

When we visited the studio of Gonzales, the potter, Henry disappeared into the main house and returned just as we were strolling through the courtyard on our way out. He was wiping his mouth on his shirttail as he trotted to catch up. Apparently, he didn't trust us to wait for him.

"Well, there you are!" I said. "Looks as though someone showed you the kitchen."

He shrugged. Walking beside us, he seemed smaller than he had in the confines of the car, and rather listless, like a clown who'd stayed on stage too long. Worried, maybe, about his fee?

"You get a rakeoff from what the tourists buy?"

"Rakeoff?"

"A percentage."

"Rakeoff," he murmured. "I learn from the tourists. At least I try. I learn from the movies, too."

He had either evaded the question or lost it in the digression, so I tried a different tack. "What's this tour going to cost us?"

He pulled himself up grandly. "Oh, Señor, whatever you wish!" Had he been one iota less cheerful, I might have mistaken his solicitude for sarcasm. His brown eyes watched his words on our faces.

"A *tostón?*" I teased, and Henry laughed, a bit unsurely, to let us know he expected more than fifty centavos.

"Where now?" I asked when we reached the car.

"You should see the studio of my friend, Juan Rodrigo. He is an artist. He has a beautiful house." He intimated that we could appreciate it in a way that others of less sensitivity and taste could not, and that it was not usually on the tour. How could we resist?

"Fine," I said. "Let's go."

"It's hard to get to." Hesitating, he surveyed the street. "You go — " he broke off, lapsing inarticulate, and fell to scribing angles and hairpins in the air with his hand. Then he held one palm up for my keys. "Maybe I better drive."

He was. . . what? Eleven? Twelve? Jack and I laughed. Henry chimed in, shrugging off the refusal.

As we pulled away, I asked him if he had driven many tourists' cars.

"Yeah. Sure. Twice. This one old lady she was real plastered" (that from the movies, no doubt) "and this old man was a *maricón*, a . . ." he faltered in search of the word, "a . . . sissy?" He looked at us meaningfully. We nodded. "He was from Canada. He took me to eat at the Carousel and said I could have anything I wanted," he went on evenly, his features calm. "I didn't know then he was a sissy so I just had some soup because I didn't have much hunger. I showed him the Teatro Juárez then he said he wanted to take me to his room at the Motel Guanajuato because he liked boys and he never had any of his own and he wanted to take my picture." While Henry rambled blithely onward, the progression of his tale made me apprehensive. "I didn't know what he wanted. I asked if I could drive and he said yes. He had a new Chevrolet. A real nice car, with these buttons on the seat and

it went up and down with a motor and *airacondicionado*. It
was fun to drive. When we got to his room I was going to ask
if he needed a. . . one of those guys who drive?"

"Chauffeur?" Dorothy put in quickly.

"Yeah. But he tried to *kiss* me!" Henry made a gagging
sound then looked at us. "I beat him up."

I stared at him.

"I did!" he said, laughing. "I hit him in the head with a
Fanta bottle and he cried."

Before we could register shock, he swung forward and
began a casual discourse on the facade of the Teatro Juárez
which appeared ahead, changing subjects so smoothly that
I wondered if the incident he described and the information he was presently giving didn't assume equal signifi-
cance in his mind. At that moment, he seemed more like a
dwarf than a boy.

Later, after we treated him to a lunch of tacos and Coke
in our hotel, Jack paid him a hundred pesos for his services
during the morning. He seemed happy with the fee — it
came to a little over eight dollars at the current rate of
exchange.

"How long will you be here?"

When Jack replied six months, he beamed.

"Are you staying in the hotel the whole time?"

I told him we'd find a house.

"I'll do it for you!" he declared, then dashed out the
door before we could protest.

When we came out of the dining room the next morning, Henry was fidgeting on the lobby's old Victorian
couch, seated directly under a huge painting which depicted, in grotesque, Rivera-like figures, the uprising which led
to the burning of the local granary during the Revolution.
To our surprise, he wore a dark blue suit coat, a dirty white
shirt joined at the collar by a clip-on bow-tie the same

coagulated color as the background in the painting. He still had on jeans and sandals, and we couldn't have said for certain that he had bathed, but seated on that red divan, he looked like an impoverished salesman all decked out for that one big closing that'd put him on his feet.

"I got a real nice place for you!" he yelped before we could say hello. "Real nice. The rent is high, but it's a real, real nice place!"

Jack eyed him skeptically — he had called the Tourist Office before breakfast and had been told nothing was available.

"How high is high?" I asked.

"Four thousand eight hundred pesos a month." He watched a bit fearfully as we calculated — about $400.

"How nice is nice?" asked Dorothy.

"Well, it has a place for sunbathing. Then there's three bedrooms, and three bathrooms — all indoors. Fireplaces in every room." He paused, scanning his imaginary catalogue, then glanced up at Midge and Dorothy, slyly. "Oh, yeah. Electric stove and oven."

Midge and Dorothy rustled, traded glances of surprise to discover he knew their minds. His ability to second-guess us made me uneasy; I felt that my prejudices, desires and tastes were so predictable that a child could manipulate me.

"Does it have a roof?" Jack asked.

"Oh, *sí*, Señor, one for every room," shot back Henry.

I smiled. "And what's your fee?" I half-expected him to say "whatever you wish," but that was all before the coat and tie.

"It's. . ." he waved, then shrugged. "Ten percent of one month," he pronounced finally. "Four hundred and eighty pesos."

He offended me. My indignation passed, though, when I saw that I had presumed he had no right to ask for anything but a boy-sized charity. What the hell — why not pay

him what we'd have to pay an agent? Henry was a marvelous example of resourcefulness. And his attempts to sell
himself charmed me because he always seemed to let us
know he was aware that his devices were transparent.

Glancing at the others, I saw that they too had bridled.

"It's a deal. If we like the house." I jumped into the
silence to override their tacit veto. I offered my hand — he
took it, grinning. His palm was sticky.

"In advance." His cheeks quivered.

I smiled. "You mean upon acceptance?"

"Yeah. When you take it."

Jack drove us up from the tunnel into the southern,
affluent end of town and onto still another plaza.

"How'd you know about this place?" I asked.

"My sister worked there once."

The day was clear and mild — the mountain air always
seemed to wash the sunlight thin, leaving the shadows cool
— but Henry's coat was blotched with sweat in the armpits
and his forehead glistened. Straining forward with his arms
crossed over the dashboard, his heels pumping against the
floor, and his lips struggling to control a perpetual grin, he
looked as if he might be enjoying some of the same feeling
I had as a boy riding on the bow of my uncle's sailboat.

Driving on, we were impressed with the neighborhood.
Because of the high walls topped with shards of glass, we
couldn't see many homes, but once, under an archway, two
palace-sized doors decked with scrollwork had been tugged
open, disclosing a courtyard with potted geraniums and
cacti in bloom. Near a spouting fountain two boys about
Henry's age were spinning tops on the tiled floor of the
courtyard while three maids in black and white uniforms
were setting places around a huge pink cake centered on a
banquet table. From a tree limb nearby hung a huge
piñata, a red donkey with green hooves and yellow ears.

"Straight ahead," Henry coaxed with barely concealed impatience after Jack pulled over so Midge could take a snapshot of the scene.

We liked Henry's house. Standing at the rear of a court-yard cluttered with tangled vines and stone statuary, it was less palatial than others in the neighborhood, but ideal, giving us both, as couples, a maximum of privacy under the same roof. The landlady, Señora Espinosa, lived in a house at the opposite end of the large garden. We learned later that we rented what had been the servants' quarters when her family, of silver-mining management stock, had kept the estate in the grand style of the neighborhood before the mines had flooded. Since then the quarters had been renovated for tourists.

"See, see," Henry persisted as we toured the rooms. "It's very nice, right?"

Señora Espinosa was an elephantine woman with a plodding walk that made me impatient to follow behind or beside her. She spoke no English so Henry interpreted for us until he finally understood that we wanted to negotiate with our neophyte Spanish, at which point he began to compliment our abominable accents. Señora Espinosa's face was as responsive as a pie pan. She showed the house slowly, neither praising its virtues nor damning its faults. I sensed that renting her property was beneath her dignity, and when I tried to bargain with her, she remained fixed in her price.

"This is the first time this house has been empty in two years," Henry piped in as we filed out of the house and into the courtyard. "She was going to the Turismo to rent it today. It would've gone — " he snapped his fingers — "just like that."

I gave him a fatherly scruff on the head.

"It's a very nice house, Henry," Dorothy told him.

"*Gracias,*" he crowed when I handed him a wad of peso notes. "You need a maid?"

I glanced at the others. "I don't know. We haven't thought about it."

"I'll come back tomorrow and see. I'd help you carry in from the car, but I have to go. *Hasta mañana.*" He vanished in a flash.

We decided against a maid on the grounds of privacy. Too, Jack and I were on pinch-penny sabbaticals and keeping up the house would at least give us purpose and discipline. Henry accepted our decision with a tiny, ironic smile flickering about his lips, as though he'd never wholly understand the queer notions of gringo tourists.

I hated to leave him empty-handed. "But in the U.S. it's a custom to let young men of your age and ambition do odd jobs here and there."

"Good. I can wash the car, take the señoras to the market, take your mail and keep your wood stacked."

I hesitated. "We'll see."

Later it bothered me that I had appeared to retract the offer when he accepted it. Maybe I only felt I had to check with the others, I thought. I mentioned it while we sat on our new terrace, feeling expansive under a sky which — at an altitude of over seven thousand feet — seemed to hang its stars just above our heads. Below us in the valley the lights of the town glimmered, and the peals of church bells floated slowly up the hillside toward us.

"Fine with me," Jack said. "Within limits, course."

We were silent a moment, then Dorothy chuckled. "I wish he wouldn't call me Señora. It makes me feel like going on a diet."

"It makes me feel my age," Midge put in. "You know," her tone shifted suddenly, "I don't really trust him." Her comment sounded like a challenge, as though she wanted to be argued out of the notion, but we all kept silent. I chalked up my reluctance to speak for him to the altitude — we were all deliciously languid — but I think her confession voiced all our unspoken reservations.

So the next morning we acquired a houseboy. Henry was to work half of each weekday. His school had been on a two-shift schedule due to crowding for so long he couldn't remember ever attending whole days there.

As his first chore, he scrubbed the car and wiped the water streaks, even giving careful attention to the wheel wells and rims — a consummate performance. I wondered, though, if what I presumed to be conscientiousness was only respect for the car, a Mercedes I had recently bought used.

For the next few weeks he ran errands and did basic maid's work about the house. But gradually he shied away from physical labor. He still washed the car far more often than I thought necessary, but since he told me that he had shined shoes when he was "little," I hadn't asked him to perform any valet's services out of respect for his pride. Eventually, though, even his assigned duties such as carrying out the garbage got only his perfunctory attention.

Yet he didn't seem to be taking advantage of us; rather, he gradually elevated himself to more important duties, as if pursuing some private, long-term strategy. He talked us into letting him change our money at the bank, buying our liquor, picking up our mail at the post office. Because Dorothy thought it might be useful to him some day, she was teaching him to type. Soon he was addressing our envelopes, and once I let him take a letter by dictation in Spanish to a friend of ours in Cuernavaca.

At the market, he helped the women bargain, showed them which stall keepers were dishonest (so he said) and which gave good measure. (Was he their agent? To this day,

I don't know.) For a while he carried their shopping bags, but one day two boys Henry's size but younger appeared, apparently retainers of his, and carted the bags away. It bothered Dorothy to see two strange boys scurrying away with their groceries, so she told Henry that they could've carried the bags themselves if the bags were too heavy for him. He grimaced, she said, like a *maitre d'* watching a customer use a dirty plate as an ashtray.

"It's ok," he grumbled. "You know me."

I laughed at her description. The boys had come promptly to the door; the contents of the bags were in order, so they need not have feared. Yet it occurred to me that we did not know Henry. I had asked him his last name once, but I couldn't be certain he said Gómez.

I quizzed him over toast and coffee. "Where would I go if I had to find you sometime when you weren't here?" He told me; I wrote the address on a napkin. Did he have brothers and sisters? Sensing an interrogation, he grew stiff, respectful. Yes sir, he did. Four brothers and three sisters, all older. Most were married.

"That makes you the baby of the family, then."

He winced, then looked down at his toast to hide his face. At the time I paid little attention, registering it as simple irritation from being called a "baby," but it could have passed for unhappiness. Having never seen anything in his face except several varieties of precociousness (all self-conscious), I was surprised at this relatively unguarded display of feeling.

And his father?

"He was killed in the mines." His eyes fixed on his toast, discouraging my prying.

After he left to carry out the trash, I felt cynical to doubt his story, but I wasn't really satisfied. I remembered he had said that his sister once worked for Señora Espinosa, so at my first opportunity I told her we had employed him and wished to know more about him. We were standing in the courtyard. She explained in patient, non-idiomatic Spanish that he was a good worker but added nothing more while I stood expectantly beside her. I wondered if her reticience was due to some reservation touching on Henry himself.

"His family is large?"

"*Si, claro.*" (What family isn't?) "He and his sister live with his aunt and uncle and their six children."

"What a pity the father's dead," I murmured.

"*Qien sabe?* Perhaps so. He went north years ago." His mother, she said, lives in Leon and works in a shoe factory. She lives with another man, and they have many children.

He lied, I thought. But the lie was pathetically unnecessary, and the irony of that touched me. The disparity between the squalor of his real situation and his own sense that it would not be enough to capture someone's sympathy reached me. We never spoke of his family again.

Old Gutiérrez — we used to see him taking the goats into the high ridges behind the town where they grazed on the clumps of grass still green from the rainy season. Occasionally when we walked into the hills we ran across him, his two dogs, and the goats perched on the steep hillside like something shoved up high on a shelf. He would be hunkering in the shade of a boulder, either whittling on a chunk of wood or staring off across the flats toward Irapuato where the factories oozed tiny streams of smoke into a pale blue sky.

You wouldn't have found his photograph among a collection depicting the simple dignity of the agrarian patriarch. Too much of the texture and color of those reddish clay hills had passed into his cheeks, barren and eroded. He never failed to return our wave with a tip of his floppy hat, and when he murmured, we saw that he was toothless. The

way his mouth receded seemed to make him too close to
death to be regarded as any symbol of the immortal spirit
of the *campesino.*

Children thought him ill-tempered. From our terrace we
saw a clutch of them pelt him with clods from behind a wall
in retaliation for the tongue-lashing he had given them for
teasing his dogs. But he was on good terms with the adults
of the neighborhood. We learned from Señora Espinosa
that even though he was not gregarious or even sociable,
he was likewise not considered a misanthropic hermit.
Because he spent much of his spare time carving gifts for
his neighbors out of wood, they liked him, but he had no
intimate friends.

For years he labored in the mines, she said, but was
known as The Lawyer Without Books because, though
unschooled, he had devoted much effort to demanding
that his former saddlemates — they had ridden with
Obregón — deliver as officials of local government what
they had promised as revolutionaries. He felt they had
betrayed the people; he had no qualms about airing his
opinion, and his unpopularity resulted in two assassination
attempts. I must have looked alarmed, for Señora Espinosa
quickly gestured to dismiss it. That was long ago, she went
on. Even before his first wife died. Only more recently, he
had remarried, a girl of eighteen, but. . . (surely I could
guess the rest?)

"She left?"

"*Si.* His only son from his first wife took her."

Since then he had confined his social activity to presenting his neighbors with these gifts — she indicated a tableau
in wood propped atop a cabinet in her kitchen, the object
which had inspired our chat. I had admired it, thought it
remarkable for its elegant simplicity, a masterpiece, really, of
primitive folk art. She tried to explain with some difficulty

that she thought his carving could be traced to his turmoil
— he did not like his love for his neighbors, I think she
said. She felt that his "fellow feeling" overflowed in wood
because he had damned it up elsewhere.

Not quite as big as a card table, the tableau depicts three
figures seated on a balcony: Señora Espinosa, another
woman (her sister), and a dog. Both women look a little
bored and indolent, but comfortably so, as though they
had just finished *comida* and were watching some pleasant
but unstimulating production by a troupe of amateur
actors. While their hand fans poise before their faces, the
dog squats on his haunches between them, his head tilted
to the right, his hind leg cocked just above his ear, on the
verge of scratching a flea. The piece is distinguished for the
suggested motion it contains and, above all, for the drollery
that pervades it. From it, I'd have said old Gutierrez was
fond of the Señora in a roguish, teasing way.

"He does not do so well anymore," she remarked suddenly. "His eyes are growing weak, he tires more quickly. I
think he knows it, too."

Henry overheard me discussing the carving, and when I
led the others down to Señora Espinosa's kitchen, he
trailed along, curious. He looked a little bewildered while
we admired the piece, but then later approached me, leaning against the desk where I was working on an article for
an educational journal.

"Senor Gutiérrez's picture — you'd buy something like
that?"

I told him yes, if it was as good as that one.

"Why?"

"Because it has. . ." I fumbled, then lapsed into arts-and-
crafts club language. "Well, it has character. Maybe you're
too young. It captures the spirit of Señora Espinosa and her
sister. It's funny, too."

"Funny?" Henry looked astonished.

"Yes. The dog."

Henry squinted in puzzlement; the humor escaped him. "But you'd pay money for something like that?"

I grew cautious — we had come to know our Henry well.

"Perhaps. It depends."

He thanked me and wandered off. The following day he presented me with a little statuette carved from a blondish wood with a dark grain, like oak. It was the figure of a thin and very old woman, with her spine curved forward, her hair flowing down her back, and her arms pressed against her sides. Her left hand held a fish, while her right gestured toward it. Her broad, flat nose was distinctly Indian; she smiled widely but not mirthfully. One foot was broken off near the instep, a thumb was missing, and a knot in the wood near the base of the skull had been too tough for the carver to manage, so the contours at that point converged into it; had the carver been more alert he might have utilized the knot as a feature of the hair style. An interesting piece, but flawed, I told Henry.

He only shrugged. "But would you buy it?"

"If I were in the market for it, I wouldn't pay more than a dollar, I guess."

"Señor Gutiérrez did it."

"I admit that might raise the price a little. Where'd you get it?"

"I didn't steal it," he said testily.

"I didn't say you had. I was told he only did things for gifts and not to sell."

"He was going to give this to someone but decided not to."

Henry had apparently become the merchandiser for the old man's seconds. I told him I didn't want it, but perhaps it would sell in the market. Henry scurried off with it.

While we sat on the terrace watching the town return to life after siesta, we saw the old man dragging Henry back from the market, his right hand vised upon Henry's neck in a pincer-grip, bellowing curses, hobbling while his two dogs raced around them, barking frantically.

Henry struggled to ease the pressure of Gutiérrez's grip by bending over, but the old man tugged him past a knot of jeering children, then into his carpenter's shop where he released him with a violent push then slammed the door. As comical as it seemed, I was afraid for Henry; the old man's strength surprised me, but I understood how Henry had gotten the piece he had shown me — he had taken it without permission from Gutiérrez's discards.

The next day Henry announced glumly that he couldn't work for us but two hours a day for a while.

"So Señor Gutiérrez puts a higher value on his creations than his agent does," I said lightly.

"He won't sell them and he won't let others sell the ones he doesn't give away." Henry pouted. "He says they aren't any good and he doesn't want anyone to see them. But the *tourists* don't know that!" he complained, then flushed suddenly. He plopped down on a stone bench and let his legs arc slowly above the tile. "He doesn't see that when tourists spend money the whole town benefits."

The idea of Henry as a budding Jaycee made Jack laugh.

"Did you tell him you were performing a public service?"

"He says I stole them." He jerked his head toward Señora Espinosa's maid, Candelária, who was poking the nozzle of a hose into the soil of a potted plant. "But I didn't!" he hissed at her. She ignored him.

"So what did he do?"

"For three weeks I have to help him carve after he brings the goats home." He sighed. "It means I will lose a lot of money." His eyes grew round, doleful. He wanted recompense.

"Look on the bright side of it," Jack offered playfully. "You might talk him into letting you take some tourists through his workshop."

Henry slid off the bench, eyes gleaming. I was surprised he hadn't thought of it himself. "Yeah. I will tell him I want the whole world to see how great he is."

A month earlier this blatant opportunism would have amused us. Now we witnessed it in embarrassed silence, and I wondered if we hadn't encouraged it all along.

Some mornings, Dorothy and Midge sunbathed on the roof. Both are on the downhill side of forty; they're avid weight-watchers and exercisers and they wore what Mexicans in the provinces consider to be racy attire — bikinis. They had the habit of turning themselves as if on a spit, untying their halters while lying prone. Had this been a public place they would have made concessions to the Mexican sense of decorum, but only one or two houses up the hill behind us allowed a view onto our roof and they looked uninhabited, like summer homes for the wealthy. An old church a block behind the house stood higher on the hill. It was said to be undergoing renovation, but no one worked there.

A couple days after Henry's run-in with the old man, when I went up on the roof Dorothy and Midge said they thought someone was watching them from the bell tower of the church. I stole a glance and caught the flash of reflected sunlight. Maybe you should sell tickets, I joked, but they were justifiably irritated at the intrusion on their privacy. I told them I'd take a closer look through my binoculars.

I looked in my desk drawer, then rummaged through the tool box in the utility room, but no binoculars. I stepped out into the courtyard because I thought maybe Henry might've left them there. He liked to look through the wrong end at things, sometimes at his feet or a free hand. Not there. I thought of asking him, then remembered he had left on an errand.

I trudged up the hill toward the church very slowly, keeping in sight of the tower. I was hoping that before I got there he'd see me and vanish. I tried to minimize his boyish voyeurism by telling myself that the desire to see a woman nude was strong at his age (and any other), but my argument didn't keep me from feeling disappointed.

After I picked my way through the stacks of tile in the churchyard, I looked up to see the front lenses of the glasses protruding over the parapet of the bell tower's landing. I hadn't taken a dozen more steps when two boys slipped through the doors to my front, spied me, gasped, took off running and vanished through an archway. Maybe Henry wasn't up there, I thought, because he didn't run with the pack.

A winding staircase mounted up to the tower. Standing in the stairwell, I saw light from the landing dimly working its way down through cobwebs strung across the well.

The fetid air was rank with turds and decaying rodents. On the wall by the first turn of the stairs someone had scrawled *La Puta Marta* with a charcoaled stick beside a crude pictograph of female genitalia; the stairs were littered with cigarette butts. As I craned my head upward, I could hear a faint murmur and a giggle. I took the stairs one at a time, clumping loudly, because I wasn't really sure of what to do, save give them a scare that might guarantee our future privacy. As I neared the top their voices grew almost intelligible, but I didn't stop to hear what they were saying.

When I pulled myself up onto the landing, Henry was leaning against the bell housing with a cigar box in one hand, chattering to another boy who was peering through the binoculars. When Henry saw me, he shouted something in Spanish; the other boy whirled, knocking the box from Henry's hand and spewing the coins inside it all over the landing, then he dropped the binoculars and raced for the stairwell. Henry froze, mouth agape, but when I moved toward him he began circling, keeping the waist-high bell housing between us. I must have looked murderous, for he spun, snatched up the box and stiff-armed it out to me, his hand shaking.

"Here's the money!" he shouted. "Please take it! I didn't look myself, I swear I didn't!"

I fired him. Looking back, I see he thought his protest that he hadn't looked exonerated him. He didn't understand that his looking was excusable but that his pandering violated our relationship so that we could no longer trust him.

We saw little of him for the next month. He always found an obvious and pathetic pretext for ducking into a store or crossing a street, and only once did we come near enough to exchange greetings, and he murmured softly with averted eyes. We learned from Señora Espinosa, however, that he had served out his sentence and wormed his way into an apprenticeship with the old man, who apparently thought that forcing Henry into the daily discipline of learning a craft would not only punish but also tame him. According to Señora Espinosa, the old man was trying, through Henry, to regain the son who had betrayed him. I think she would've called their relationship symbiotic: the old man was going blind; Henry would be his eyes, and in return he could learn something useful.

It disturbed me, though, to think of the old man's deception. Approaching the age when he knew death to lie in the simplest fixtures of everyday life, he would naturally desire to pass himself on through his craft, and for him to imagine that this little opportunist might have any interest in anything requiring discipline or integrity would be gross self-deception. A greed of its own kind, a greed for immortality.

One afternoon late as I was coming up the street, I happened to look into the doorway of the old man's workshop. Henry was seated high on a stool, his back to the door, bent over something before him, his right hand clutching a wooden mallet. Gutiérrez stood beside him, explaining, it seemed, something about the object on the bench. His left arm was draped around the boy's neck. The afternoon light slanted so that a large block of it fell across the bench and enveloped their figures in yellow rays vibrant with motes. If you didn't know Henry, I thought, that scene might make a poignant rendering of rich contrasts — young and old, life and death, innocence and knowledge. Knowing Henry, the contrasts were insidiously ironic: Henry the wise, the old man the innocent.

One morning just after dawn I saw them coming up the hill with the goats, the old man thumping along with his cane, teasing Henry while the boy stared brightly into his face, the very paragon of a youngster eager for his father's attention. *Buenos días*, I called out loudly. The old man waved his cane. Henry quickly looked ahead, but I could see my greeting had accomplished its intended effect — he knew I had my eye on him.

That afternoon I saw him leading tourists through the shop. From the terrace, I could see his gestures, could almost hear his spiel and I thought with embarrassment of how they'd be duped by his charm. He wore his business suit, his hair was slicked back and as he pointed with authority up and down the street before he got into their

car, they turned their heads to and fro like tennis specta-
tors.

Two days later as I sat at my morning coffee, I looked
down to see him coming along the street behind the goats.
Alone. He's gotten that far, has he? I thought. I watched
him look everywhere but up at me, knowing I was watching him. When he was directly beneath me, he looked up,
not defiantly, but simply as though he couldn't have avoided it and still have called himself a man, and when he did I
felt silly holding so large a grudge against so small a person.

"Good morning, Henry," I sang out — a bit wryly to
acknowledge our struggle.

"*Buenos días*, Senor," he murmured as he passed. It was
such a remarkable imitation of sincerity that I began to
doubt my suspicions.

Señora Espinosa told me at noon that Gutiérrez had fall-
en ill and Henry was tending to his business. This went on
for four or five days and Henry and I reached a kind of
truce through our daily greeting. I was curious to see how
long he'd hang on to the old man, for surely any profit to
be made would have to be on long terms. Only when he
led the tourists through the shop did he have contact with
them any more. Apparently he hadn't tried to pass off the
old man's seconds, either. The times must be lean for him,
I thought. Maybe he was riding on his savings, waiting for
the kill.

Soon he showed up with a shoebox under his arm.
Although immediately wary, I invited him in but led him
no farther than to the benches in the garden.

"How've you been?" I asked. He looked tired.
Depressed, maybe, or preoccupied.

"*Bien*," he said dully.

We sat a moment in an awkward silence, like two
strangers working on a conversation at a bus stop.

"Sorry to hear your friend is sick."

He nodded and stared at his scuffed shoes as his legs dangled in listless circles above the tile. He wore dusty jeans and a washed-out shirt with half the buttons missing.

"I'm sorry," he blurted out, his gaze sweeping by mine, coming back to almost touch, then skittering away. "The glasses — "

"Oh, it's all right." I was cool. With the old man close to death, Henry needed to rebuild bridges he had burned, I thought.

"You want your old job back?"

"No."

He kept shifting the shoe box he held in his lap. I reminded myself that Henry wouldn't pay a simple social call without an ulterior motive. Yet where once he pursued his con games with zest, his manner now suggested that he was fulfilling a painful duty. I wondered if his conspicuous failure to mention the contents of the box was a new approach.

"What's in the box?" I asked, feeling defeated.

He looked away. "A piece of Señor Gutiérrez's primitive folk art."

My phrase sounded absurd coming from his mouth.

"I presume it's for sale."

He avoided my gaze, eased the lid off the box with exaggerated care, then rose from the bench and carried the box like an offering to where I sat.

"It's his best work," he announced with something of his former guide's inflection.

The sculpture was couched in orange tissue paper — a figure in dark wood, of an old man. It was a sardonic self-portrait by Gutiérrez and from the quickest glance I saw the truth in Henry's claim: the detail was marvelous — items as minute as his fingernails and belt buckle had been tooled with patience and care for the highest verisimilitude.

While I inspected it Henry hovered nearby, troubled, as if afraid for it in my hands. He put his hands in his pockets then took them out.

"Yes, it's the best of his I've seen."

"How much would you give for it?" Henry asked quickly and quite unhappily. His manner irritated me; he acted as if I were a pawnbroker to whom he had just brought the last of the family jewels. I decided not to buy it under any circumstances.

"You sure it's for sale?"

"Yes, yes! How much?" He circled behind me, swatting at the flowers with his cupped palm.

"A dollar."

"Not enough." He sounded strangely troubled. He strode around beside me and pointed at the figure, his hand trembling. "Look at it! You know it's good!"

"Just how did you get this?"

He evaded my question by circling behind me again, then suddenly he collapsed onto the bench, deflated and listless.

I repeated my question to his back.

He mumbled.

"What?"

"I got it from *El Señor*." He rose from the bench and approached me, head lowered, his features twisted into a grimace. He was fighting not to cry. "How much?"

"Did he give it to you?"

"Yes."

"You're lying!"

"No!"

"Who'd he make it for?"

"For me!" He burst into sobs, tore the box from my hands, and as I watched, stunned, he dashed from the courtyard and down the street, his sobbing and his footfalls echoing after him.

I felt buoyant, billowing in pride for our Henry. That he couldn't sell the gift was a sign of a change for the better. I told the story to Dorothy, Midge, and Jack, and together we all had our hope restored. I felt vaguely guilty over having been proved a cynic, and I confessed that I didn't think Henry would've made the choice he did, although I could see him struggling over it.

Obviously he had intended to sell the present, but he must have realized that the bond with the old man amounted to a higher value than the price of the figure.

Gutiérrez died that evening, about the same hour that we were celebrating our victory over Henry. Señora Espinosa didn't tell us until morning, and we were shamefaced at the knowledge that while the neighborhood was mourning, we had sat on our terrace carousing.

Henry was missing. On the chance that he had gone into the hills to grieve, I climbed the path they took each morning with the goats and after a half hour of walking, I spotted him sitting beneath a boulder, squatting with his head between his knees, rocking slowly back and forth.

He looked up when he heard me approach and grew tense when he recognized me. He rose to his feet and with the toe of one sandal pushed dirt over a mound before him.

He looked incredibly tired; his eyes lay in bruise-colored pockets of flesh, and layers of dust and tears clotted his cheeks.

"I'm. . . terribly sorry." I was nervous and at a loss to console him. I had prepared a little speech, so I gave it: the old man hadn't died in vain, for he had passed on his craft and character to Henry; we were very proud, I said, that he hadn't sold the gift, that he had chosen to keep it.

He eyed me narrowly, looked down the mountain, then with his toe he nudged away the dirt from the mound at his feet. The figure was buried there. He had defaced it.

He turned, fell against the boulder. "I couldn't sell it," he said a moment later. "I didn't want to! If I'd sold it, I could of got some money for a doctor or medicine!" He began crying again.

I didn't know what to do, but I wanted to console him.

"Henry, why didn't you say something?"

I drew out my wallet. Astonished, he glared, then he charged at me, fists windmilling, cursing, and I had to drop my wallet and hold him at arm's length while he kicked at my shins. He struggled, then tore loose from my grip and spat at me. Angry, I grabbed for him, but he bounded down the hill out of reach.

"All you think about is money!" he yelled over his shoulder as he ran.

Domestic Help

I had just opened a Dos XX when a plum-colored VW bus slid to a halt on the road outside the knee-high wall that bordered my terrace. Out of it popped a thirtyish female in Levis and a denim shirt whose tails draped her thighs like an apron. She wore a railroad engineer's hat; her black hair was braided into a single rope which hung to her waist. Ignoring the gate, she jumped the wall. Sans bra.

"Dirk around here?" She thumbed her glasses up her nose.

"He's in Cuernavaca until tomorrow."

"Christ!" She plopped down into the low-slung chair across the table. Silent and glum, she gazed off behind me. I was about to offer her a beer when she roused herself, pulled a joint from her purse and lit it.

"I'm tired of being hassled by these bastards, man!" For an instant I thought she was confusing me with somebody else, then I guessed she was a person to whom everybody else is faceless. "I was trucking up 45 to Irapuato and this guy kept pulling beside me and honking and waving. I figured I must have met him in the city somewhere, so I grinned and waved back. Then he started doing this — " She stuck her right index finger through a hole made by her left. "So I got pissed and gave him this — " She raised her left middle finger erect in the air and slapped the back of that hand against her right palm.

During this pantomime the joint teased the varnish with a brown cannabis kiss, so I retrieved it and took a toke to play the perfect host.

"This asshole started playing all these dumbass macho games, you know, pulling in front of me and slowing down or getting beside me and trying to run me off the road. Finally I just stopped. He got out of his car and started toward me, and I tried to run the fucker down. I lost him in Irapuato."

"Friend of yours?"

"No way, Jack." The long braid swung into view then vanished behind the chair. "When I try to be friendly, some guacho thinks I'm hot for his bod. Goddamnit, I like to sit in bars and talk to people, but I always get hassled!" She leaped up and dashed to the wall. "*Quítesen!*" she yelled at two boys who were hanging around the bus. Giggling, they darted away.

"Little bastards!"

"They probably wanted to wash it."

"Hah! Come here." She beckoned to me from the wall. Beside her, I could see that the flanks of the bus sported a coat of grime in which wet fingers had written not only the usual "*Lávame!*" or "wash me!" but also the Spanish equivalents for "Kiss my cock!" "Great White Whore" and "Wanna screw?"

"They want to put more on there." She dragged off the joint then ground a good-sized roach under her toe. "Some kids did that when me and my old man were living in Guadalajara. I'm split with him now. Every morning they'd bug me to wash the car, you know, but I'd tell them to get lost, so they wrote that crap on it." She jabbed at her glasses.

"Why don't you have it washed?"

She flared. "Because they thought they could blackmail me!"

"Maybe that guy thought you were advertising," I said, taking the coward's way of joshing everybody through the rough spots.

Her squint-eyed gaze lowered my category. "I don't give a shit what they think! I didn't write it, and I'm not taking it off!"

Her shrill vow reverberated in the still air. I watched a hummingbird flit past the branches of the pepper tree we stood beneath, then across the river the stonecutters working on Fernández's new archway started up, filling the air with a steely chink of their hammers.

"I gotta go." She put her hands on her hips, then sniffed. "Jesus Christ, that river stinks!"

"Yeah. I don't notice it much anymore, though."

We watched a kind of acquatic sculpture ooze by on the gray-green water: spirals of orange peel, a watermelon rind, and a few turds of distinguishable origin bobbing inside a ring of soap bubbles.

"You'd think they'd have enough sense not to throw their garbage in the river! It really drives me wild!" She frowned. "You know, this wouldn't be a bad country if it wasn't for the Mexicans!"

I laughed before realizing she had spoken the cliché without the faintest touch of irony.

"Try going without a bra," she recommended. "Man, you know what these assholes think?"

I waited for an answer; none came. She had smoked most of the joint herself.

"What?" I prompted.

"I'm going to get a club and the next dude that hassles me is getting it in the nuts!" She stared at the car, transfixed. "You know who he reminded me of?" she asked, a little awed.

"No."

"My father."

Where I come from, that's about the point where conversation can begin. If she hadn't been on the brink of departure with the moment of intimacy slipping away as inexorably as our turd and orange peel assemblage was lilting its way downstream, we could have traded some heartfelt stuff such as names and occupations. But she was shut off, her gaze focused on the billboard slabs of bus. The rope of hair had swung over her shoulder, and she absently laid it between her breasts and stroked it over and over, the way men do their neckties. In a moment, she looked up to catch me watching her with curiosity.

"Ciao, man! Tell Dirk I'm looking for him."

When I relayed the message to my landlord and pried him for information, I learned that Vera was an expatriate American weaver who had moved to the village a few years ago with her husband and rented a house just down the road from mine. Six months prior to my coming, they had moved to Guadalajara, then divorced. The settlement had left her with some money, and now she wanted to buy the same house through one of those mysterious, quasi-legal ways that foreigners attain property in Mexico, a project Dirk was counselling her on.

Formerly a small chapel inside the walled yard of a colonial church whose larger structure had been partially destroyed by a flood earlier in the century, the property had been reconstructed into a two-bedroom dwelling by a local architect and builder according to the specifications of its present absentee owner, who was now selling it.

"Watch it!" Dirk grinned. I shrugged. Vera was too prickly for my tastes, and I was probably too watchful for hers. I told myself that I wanted to study her demon, but because there was a shortage of unattached women around the village, I'd have been fooling myself to say my interest was strictly academic. I was in Mexico to recuperate from a messy divorce; I could have used a bed partner but not a troublesome relationship.

Two days later I found Vera at the register counter in the *supermercado* having a faceoff with the proprietor's wife. Her back was to me; she was clad in huaraches, her engineer's hat, and a chartreuse bikini. Three *campesinos* in baseball caps and white shirts were perched on Coke cases near the front door, drinking Fantas as they waited for the Guanajuato bus. They were calling each other's attention to her anatomy with elbow nudges and whispers. Stock in their libido was on a bullish rampage. In provincial Mexico, ladies swim in one-piece suits of sombre colors; less modest attire invites accusations of exhibitionism and promiscuity. Vera seemed oblivious to the concept of cultural context.

"Goddamnit, I want *jamón*, not *jabón*!" she complained to the wife, whose ingenuous expression was tainted with malice.

I ambled up. "What's happening?"

"Jesus! You ask for ham and you get soap!" She jabbed a forefinger at the stack of soap bars on the counter. "What's with these people?" She glared at the wife, who was strolling toward the meat counter where her husband stood looking pointedly off into space: what Vera's jeans and baggy shirt had hidden, the bikini revealed — some very appealing proportions. Stumbling onto this stirring vision and feeling the wife bristling, even I was embarrassed.

"Maybe she's trying to tell you something."

"Soap for ham!" Vera snorted. "What the hell does that say?"

She stomped off into a huff, her audience of *campesinos* blushing like schoolgirls in the proximity of those jiggling breasts. "*Chingan sus ojos!*" she tossed over her shoulder as she breezed through the door.

Later I learned that when Vera and her husband had lived here, she had been known to the locals as an obnoxious, hard-to-please *gringa*. But now, as a liberated divorcee, she was a threat to the moral order: she didn't pull the drapes to her windows off her bedroom balcony; she picked up hitchhikers to and from Guanajuato; she held afternoon salons with as many as four males; she drank alone with men at night; she cursed, smoked, displayed her body. My maid Belén gave me sidelong glances of reproach when Vera dropped by to chat and would disappear so that I had to serve Vera myself.

But if Vera was out to corrupt anyone's innocence, it wasn't mine. Her sexuality was an enigma; she spoke to me in a way which could have come from the guy who shared my drafting table in high school mechanical drawing. She didn't flirt, and I felt rejected, even though I wasn't sure I'd want to follow through. She talked about her former husband, her "old man," with resentment, confiding in me that he was "hung up on status and money" and "a lousy fuck." A less bitter inflection might have implied she was looking for a good one, but at her parties she never paired off and she never touched or spoke to a man in a way that anyone from her own country would have taken as a mating signal. Maybe her divorce had stunned her, I thought. She seemed asexual, so guarded around everyone that she left no room for play. It helped my ego to remember that.

I went to her parties to get a handle on her and to meet people — she seemed to know all the artists and artisans within a hundred-mile radius. Invariably present were good dope and liquor and dreary talk about events in Republican America. Vera was full of shallow and inconsistent opinions that she aired in a vocabulary whose most persistent imagery was scatalogical. She would rail against the mildest disagreement or predictably take offense at a remark whose ambiguity would have given a more secure person the option of reading it benignly.

Usually she got into shouting matches with her guests, occasionally over politics, but, as a hobbyhorse, that ran a poor second to "hassles" like those she had described on our first meeting. One afternoon she baited an American friend of hers who lived with a Mexican law student. "Vera, you can't act the way you did at home because they look at it from a macho point of view. Believe me, I know." Helen gave her lips a sorrowful twist. A party was in progress, but the three of us were seated around her coffee table. Formerly the chapel's sanctuary, the living room still had the original stained-glass panels on its west walls, and the sunlight transferred the Madonna, Ruth, and the crucified Christ onto the table and the interior walls beyond. "Jaime will never marry me now, you know. Because he's slept with me. I'm — " she hesitated, her three tequila cocktails bringing her to the point of crying, then caught herself. "I'm *soiled*. His word. It's absurd, but there it is. I got drawn into a relationship with him before I knew what these things mean to them. Read Paz. A *gringa* and her money are a humiliation and they have to save face by dominating and hurting." She pressed her palms against her face and rubbed her eyes; her hands were the blue of Ruth's robe. "You can't ignore their customs and not pay a heavy price. I know, I'm telling you. You really should bend a little before they break you. They can do it."

"Crap! What can they do?"

"Jaime says — oh, never mind!"

"Says what, huh?"

"He says there's not a court in the state that would convict some guy for raping you. He'd doubt if there'd even be an arrest. To them you're a slut."

Vera blushed angrily. "Well, I'm not like you. I'm not a goddamn geisha bowing and scraping and speaking only when I'm spoken to. I know what guys like Jaime expect from women, but they ought to have some respect for my lifestyle. I ought to be able to live the way I want without a lot of greasy gauchos slobbering all over me because I offer them a ride or because I want to sit in a bar or because I don't wear a goddamn brassiere!"

Agreed. But I couldn't think of her as a revolutionary acting on principle: I thought of her as a spoiled and impetuous thirty-year-old child, a nigh-onto unanimous opinion. When people gathered without her, they spent hours complaining about her, laughing at her, trading anecdotes with grim pleasure. Usually someone said, "For God's sake! Let's talk about something else!" But within minutes backsliders to that vow indulged in monologues about her lack of manners, her subjectivity, her outrageous treatment of her maids, her provocative behavior. Why? I wondered.

I decided that exasperated pity explained my interest. She carried a chip on her shoulder large enough to break her back, and that dedication to self-defeat aroused a paternal instinct, maybe. She couldn't exchange money at the bank without enduring a humiliation of some sort; the simple act of getting a station attendant to gas up her car became a war between sexes and cultures.

And the war had a home front. She changed maids weekly; either she fired them in a fit of pique or they quit in one. She expected young girls from village families to have the mechanical savvy of an Edison, the dedication of a Schweitzer and the energy of a burro — all for a few pesos a day.

But she met her match in Carmen. Weighing about twelve stone, Carmen had black hair streaked with platinum and a mouth full of gold inlays. About the village she was a queen of domestics, and she came into Vera's employ when departing winter residents passed her on. A fine cook and an experienced housekeeper unintimidated by machinery, Carmen shouted at Vera to keep off her floors and yanked her arm out of the refrigerator if she caught Vera rummaging about for a snack. She filched from Vera's stores and didn't bother to hide it. Vera fired her twice but hired her back because her replacements were so incompetent, she claimed, and because by then she had exhausted or irritated all the other maids. Tough and irascible, Carmen seemed to thrive on their mutual agitation.

Carmen's husband was a free-lance contractor who owned an old flatbed International; he and his small crew did construction for the architect who restored the old ruins about the village. He dressed like the more or less prosperous businessman he was, in dark slacks, white shirt open at the collar, only his straw hat revealing his *campesino* heritage. Unlike others who had risen, Tomás had kept the respect of the villagers by not moving into Guanajuato; he had not forsaken his old *amigos*, and after work he still bent elbows with his work crew at the *cantina*. Elected as a delegate to the provincial parliament, for all appearances he had a rich and tranquil life, wading placidly through rooms choked with his seven children or serving tequila and *atole* at their birthday parties attended by *Mexicano* and *gringo* alike. He might have lived forever with peace and *dignidad* had he not gotten tangled up with Vera.

Naturally, Vera hired him to complete the job left by the previous owners on her courtyard. Naturally, they had to have long conversations in the evenings, each with a beer, Vera chain-smoking Fiestas, Tomás nibbling *pepitos*, only the coffee table between them and no one else in the house, Carmen having left to care for the aforementioned children.

Naturally, Carmen was less than pleased about the arrangement. As if to disarm her jealousy, Vera praised Tomás to her face, citing his resourcefulness, his ingenuity, his generosity, his conscientiousness. "Oh, Carmen, I don't know what I'd do without Tomás to take care of things! He's a real buddy!" she gushed, as though talking about a grandfatherly handyman and loyal retainer, never calling attention to his great energy, his strong good looks or his smile. Though like Carmen he was in his mid-forties, his body was lithe and agile, his muscles wiry. Streaks of grey mellowed his temples and salted his moustache. He gave off an aura of wisdom whose reality might be questioned considering how this volatile triangle eventually collapsed.

Gossip linked them as lovers, but I never drew a conclusion until one night when Helen and I were at Vera's. Obsessed with her house plans as only somebody building an air castle can be, Vera now wanted to enclose the courtyard, partition off interior space, add closets and shelves. She had enough mental blueprints to keep Tomás in consultation until death might them part. She rhapsodized about his intelligence, his capacity to understand her, his intuitive genius, and so forth until Helen and I began to pass covert glances of surprise.

Tomás came to the door. When Vera ushered him into the room, I caught his fleeting expression of disappointment before it quickly dissolved behind a mask. He was polite but slightly embarrassed, passing out smiles like a perfect ambassador between sips of the beer she served him.

"Oh, Tomás! Tell them about the *ratón!*"

"*Bueno.*" Smiling dutifully, he related with detectable reluctance how Vera had been plagued nightly by a large rat which had been coming in and —

"Tomás built the most clever trap I've ever seen!" Vera bubbled. "It was a box made of wire and when *el ratón* went in to get the bait the door closed behind him. Tomás took him out into the desert and let him go!" Implicit was Tomás's compassion for wee beasties, but I guessed it was the only usuable trap for a rat as big as the one Vera then formed between her hands.

"*El ratón* was really *grande*, eh Tomás? Oh, it was a big mother!" she chattered, turning to us.

"*Si, muy grande. El jefe.*" Tomás grinned dryly, conqueror of rats.

As Vera developed her theme of man-saves-woman-from-mouse, Tomás got nervous. Later, while Vera was walking him to the door, I realized that she had talked for half an hour without once bristling.

"God, he's *such* a nice guy!" she burst out on returning. "He doesn't hassle me. He doesn't come on like a *pachuco* or anything."

I privately agreed, but my jealousy made me notice that his reserved exterior hadn't completely hidden an id quivering like a tub of sticky Jell-O beneath it.

"It's obvious you're in love with him, anyway." Helen sounded irritated.

"Oh, gosh no!" Vera set the braid swinging behind her

chair. "He's like a big brother. I trust him." She laughed. "If he told me jumping off a cliff was good for me, I'd probably do it."

"I noticed you had your bus washed. You got it bad, kid."

She grinned at me. "And that ain't good?"

"Hardly," Helen said grimly.

"Hey, really! I don't love him. He's my contractor. He's Carmen's husband. I sure don't want another," she said with less levity.

Helen cocked her head.

"No kidding! I don't want anybody to think — "

"They already do. You know you didn't swear when he was here?"

"Tomás respects me. Anyway, so what?"

Helen slumped on the couch and shielded her breasts with crossed arms. "I suppose you're happy too, huh?"

"Sure!" Vera blurted without thinking. After a moment she frowned and began chewing on her thumbnail. Helen's attitude annoyed me. I liked this new Vera, even if I wasn't responsible for the change. I winked at her.

"Happy, Vera? Shame on you."

She grinned. Helen got up and brushed her palms across her hips as though to clean them. "Don't be a goddamn fool, Vera! If you listen to him you're going to be sorry!"

After Helen left, Vera stayed pensive.

"I can't be in love with Tomás."

"You mean you've got proof to the contrary?"

"Well, he's married to Carmen," she said, pained. She turned, and light passing through the windows laid a blotch of red across her torso. "Also, I've never been in love." She raised her fingers and rubbed the eye closest to me.

"What about Jerry?"

"I was twenty-seven and I had never had an offer. I

needed somebody. Not just anybody, but three out of ten would have fit the bill. He knew it would drive his Jewish parents up the wall for him to marry a wop."

"And you don't love Tomás?"

"No!" The braid whipped behind the chair. "It couldn't lead anywhere. By the way — " She leaned forward and fixed me with a look of fierce determination. "He has *never* touched me!" Oddly, her tone made this a testimony to his virtue, not hers.

"I never thought he had," I said truthfully. "But you haven't shown me anything that says you don't love him."

"Just drop it, will you?" Her hands pressed the arms of the chair. "I decided a long time ago that some people can't do it. I used to be afraid I never could, but now I've gotten used to it, and I can spend the rest of my life without it." She slipped off her glasses and pressed the heels of her hands into her eyes. "Besides, I don't see what's so great about it — it's overrated. What the hell do you care, anyway? You didn't do so hot along that line yourself."

"Touché," I agreed, to restore peace. Walking home, I wondered what stake I had in Vera's life. A soppy matchmaker in me liked the transformation in Vera from childish girl to child-like, guileless woman. All right — I was jealous, too. But I hadn't recovered enough to leap into another relationship, and the voyeur in me was glad somebody had somebody. Vera was a pathfinder, and I sat secure in the outpost waiting for her reports from the frontier.

Remembering our conversation, I thought it was a perversely bollixed situation that had Helen accusing her of loving and me trying to wring a shameful confession of it from her. The resistance of her defense proved the charge, and I was sure that poor Vera did love, but since her situation with Tomás could only be painful, she couldn't allow herself to love him, so she told herself she didn't. Trying to avoid pain by keeping sex at arm's length, she had not noticed love sneaking in.

Vera called Tomás that night and asked him to come *muy pronto* — somebody was prowling around in her courtyard. Tomás went and didn't leave until 4 A.M. A few hours later Vera discovered that Carmen had quit and had organized a boycott against her.

"For Christ's sake!" Vera complained to me. "We just talked and drank some beer so whoever it was would go away! I can't believe that Carmen really thinks Tomás is anything but a buddy to me! Why can't these goddamn people leave me alone?"

Carmen could harass Vera, but she couldn't stop Tomás from coming to Vera's house. His business was unfinished, and it would have grated on his machismo to appear cowed by Carmen. Although she was probably making life miserable for him at home, it might have been a comfort for him to know that everyone was now sure that Vera was his *querida*. Carmen's open hostility had validated the suspicion. Was he amused by the struggle between the two women? Shamed or annoyed by it? Or, worse luck to both, proud of it?

Soon after Carmen's declaration of war, I was sitting on La Pasita's balcony chewing on a *flauta* and brooding over an empty notebook when down the street came Tomás and two of his workers, walking home for *comida*. Vera's bus came abreast of them. She stopped, smiled, and beckoned, and he strolled over to the driver's window. From her gestures, I presumed their conversation to be about her house. In a moment, she smiled again, waved to his fellows, and drove off.

Deadpan, Tomás rejoined his companions, who jostled him with their elbows as they walked toward me. Their words were not distinguishable, but their intent was clear:

hey, hombre, you been getting some of that, eh? Tomás wasn't
swaggering or grinning lewdly, but the negative wag of his
head seemed calculated to imply its opposite. They disappeared beneath the balcony and emerged on my right.
Tomás had his arms about the shoulders of his *amigos.*
"You can't deny women what they want," he was saying.

Tomás seemed powerless to stop Carmen's harassment.
She invited the proprietress of the *supermercado* to join her
boycott. No sooner would Vera carry a shopping bag full of
groceries to the register than there'd be no one to take her
money. Once in anger, Vera walked away with a full bag,
but when she reached the front door, the proprietress
screamed, *Thief!* and Vera, fearing that not even an arrest
for shoplifting was beneath her enemies, dropped the bag
at the threshold.

Vera countered by making another late call to Tomás
asking for his protection from another prowler, this one
more imagined than real, I'd guess. When he showed up
but said he couldn't stay long, she gave him a silk shirt and
insisted he try it on for size. Stupidly or defiantly, Tomás
wore it home. Shortly after noon the next day as Vera was
driving on the river road toward Guanajuato, Carmen
stepped from behind a tree and into her path, carrying a
basket of wet laundry. Vera slammed on her brakes and
barely avoided running her down. The stone-cutttters working a few yards away claim their dialogue went something
like this:

"Goddamnit, Carmen! What the hell do you mean
jumping out in front of me like that! Why don't you leave
me alone?"

"You better leave my Tomás alone!"

"Listen, *Cula Gorda* — "

She got no farther than "Fat Ass." Carmen yanked the
door open and toppled Vera off the VW's high seat and

onto the ground, and when Vera got up to run, Carmen chased her, whipping her over the head with a wet shirt.

"It was the one I gave him, I think," Vera confirmed through tears the next day. She rummaged in her fishnet purse for a cigarette, then lifted the purse off the tile of my patio and slung it onto the table. It landed with a heavy clunk. Metal gleamed through the netting.

"What's in there?"

"A pistol."

"Loaded?"

"Is the Pope Catholic?" She lit her cigarette with shaking fingers.

"On safety?"

"I dunno."

I couldn't tell if her indifference was histrionics or ignorance. "Mind if I check?" Gingerly, I reached into the purse, closed my hand on metal and extracted an old army-issue .45. It wasn't on safety. "Here — " I demonstrated the procedure for her, but she barely glanced at my hands. I set the pistol on the table with the muzzle toward the terrace wall.

"Going to rob a bank?"

She snickered then stroked the braid between her breasts. "Nope," she said tightly. "I'm going to blast the next fucker who tries to lay a finger on me."

I threw up my hands in mock relief. "Oh, well! I thought maybe you were gunning for Carmen."

She didn't want to be joked out of her anger. She avoided my gaze, her eyes alternating between the pistol and the terrace wall. "Her too, if she crosses me," she said darkly.

"At least let me teach you how to handle it, ok?" No response. "I'll keep it here, and — "

"No!" She sprang to the edge of the chair as if I had moved to take the pistol, which I hadn't. "It's the only protection I have now!"

"Oh, come on, Vera! You're being melodramatic."

"Oh yeah? You'll see!"

"What?"

"When they find out I can't call Tomás any more — " A sob choked off her sentence, then she clenched her teeth. "You know," she went on after a moment, "the guys who think I'm a slut, the ones Jaime says can rape me without worrying about the law."

"You don't think that's paranoia?"

She shook her head vigorously.

"How about the police?"

She grimaced with disgust.

"If you're scared, you can stay here." I delivered this line with as brotherly an expression as I could muster. Vera looked as if she might go for the pistol.

"Oh, sure!" she muttered. Craven fear kept me from saying that a deranged woman with a loaded pistol was about as desirable a lover as a porcupine on speed.

"I'm sorry," she relented. She laid her face in her hands and wept quietly for awhile, then with an effort, she jerked herself upright. "Goddamnit, man! You know, I really. . . liked him! It's a shame that bitch has her hooks in him so deep." She pulled a tissue from her purse and blew her nose, then gripped the wadded ball in her fist. "We called it quits."

"Carmen too much for you?"

She shrugged. "I could take it, I guess. When I told him this morning what happened between me and Carmen, he was very embarrassed. He said — " She sighed, hugely. "He said he was sorry for all the trouble our friendship had caused me. He didn't want to see me hurt. He recommended another contractor in Guanajuato. I know he was trying to do the right thing, but I lost my head."

"You got mad?"

"Very." She looked away. "I said some ugly things. Like that Carmen had cut off his *cojones*," she went on painfully. "I called him a *pendejo*. He was very shocked. At least it proves one thing — " She gritted her teeth until a threatening wave of weeping had passed. "You don't say things like that to people if you love them. I'd give anything to take those words back."

A *pendejo* can't get it up. Literally, he "dangles." In a culture where virility is the supreme male virtue, it's a terrible insult; from a woman, it's a devastating humiliation. When I saw Tomás two nights later, he looked as if he still smarted from its sting. I was at Hernando's nursing a Dos XX while observing Tomás and three buddies who were getting plastered on tequila they chased with beer. The atmosphere was poisonous. Tomás passed within hailing distance on his way to the can but didn't hail me. He wasn't in the mood to dispense any diplomatic smiles. One of his companions was Carmen's brother; between lapses in the million-decibel ranchero music on the juke, I could hear him goading Tomás: ". . . and so Paco says to her, 'However you like it, Señora!'" A spray of cackling burst from the trio as the brother-in-law made barking sounds and slapped Tomás's back. Tomás sat gray as a stone, staring at the ashtray, reaching out now and then to fill his shot glass with tequila, which he then tossed down without benefit of ritual lime and salt.

Rancheros on the juke lamented in waltz-time: *In you my darling I had such confidence that in the end I remained unwed. And now I toss myself into a sea of forgetfulness. . . I fling myself to the vices. . . I get drunk, Fulanita, to see if I can forget.* The brother-in-law pantomimed a striptease, cupping hands under breasts and rolling his eyes, then he jammed the point of his tongue into his cheek and tried to talk, winking at the other two until they slapped at the table and bent over to hold their guts with laughter. Their jokes must have had an especially cruel irony — I was fairly sure Tomás had never had the rich *gringa* whose loss they seemed to be teasing him about.

"*Cállete!*" Tomás shouted at last. They all shut up. Weaving, he got up from the table and glared at them. Then he turned and bumped his way through the empty chairs toward the back, knocking his shoulder once against a pillar.

Discretion and foresight make good ambassadors. I left before Tomás came out of the restroom. Hours later, it seemed, I dreamed I was walking along the river road when Tomás's old flatbed came rattling toward me, wandering all over the road. I stepped off to give the truck a wide berth. Tomás was driving, his companions with him, singing. As the truck passed, it backfired.

I woke with a start and lay still until I realized that the sound had been real. I leaped out of bed, dressed, dashed out my door and started running to Vera's house a couple hundred yards away. As I rounded the last bend, puffing and heaving, her house loomed out of the moonless night like a ghost ship, the roof backlit by the floodlight in the rear courtyard. A lamp in the livingroom illuminated one stained-glass panel, making the reds lurid in the darkness. I heard voices and footfalls closing on my left flank, but I didn't stop. I darted up her gravelled drive and to the door in the courtyard wall. It wasn't latched; I sailed through it and tumbled onto the patio outside her kitchen.

"Vera!" I could hear her bawling and talking incoherently. The kitchen door was locked. I hurried around the side of the house and came onto her main patio at the rear; the floodlamp cast a puddle of light in the center of the yard, leaving the back in shadows.

In the far corner I saw movement low along the wall,

convulsive and abrupt. Vera's sobs came from in the house on my right. I ran to the door leading onto the patio from the workroom, tripped over the pistol lying on the tiles and kicked it away, swung the workroom door open and plunged inside. Vera was crosslegged on the floor like a Muslim at prayer, moaning and bumping her forehead against the tiles, face in hands. I grabbed her shoulders.

"Vera!"

She looked up, then pointed into the courtyard. "Please, please, tell him I'm sorry! Oh, God! I'm sorry!"

Running toward the back wall, I hoped "he" was alive enough to hear an apology. Beside a stack of tile Tomás lay in a fetal position on his side, both hands clutching his right foot.

"*Mi pie! Ah, mi pie!*" He rocked himself and groaned.

"You all right?" Out of the corner of my eye I saw that more of Vera's neighbors had come into the courtyard and were making their way toward us.

"The whore shot my foot!" he grunted.

"She says she's sorry." It sounded absurd. I started chuckling, maybe from relief.

"*Cabrón!*" Tomás hissed.

Later when he hobbled around on crutches with a belligerent scowl, other people laughed, but not to his face. The former *gringa* mistress who had given him his ridiculous wound got off scot free — one of Jaime's lawyer friends saw that the proper palms were greased.

I checked Vera's house two or three times a day and night for the next week, but she wasn't in. She was seen driving to and from Guanajuato, so I thought she was ok, more or less.

One afternoon, her bus pulled up beside my terrace wall loaded with household goods and parts of her dismantled loom. Listlessly, she slid from the driver's seat and checked

the tires before making her way through the gate and onto
the terrace where I sat sunning.

"Hi."

She returned my greeting with a limp wave then fished a
cigarette out of an open pack lying on the table.

"Going somewhere?"

"North. Way North."

"Renewing your visa?"

"No, for good."

I raised up from my beach towel. Goodbye? I watched
her a minute to gauge her spirits. She looked very pretty.

"Like my costume?" She gestured toward the knee-
length denim skirt and the white Indian blouse decorated
with swirls of embroidery. She did a mock curtsy. "Ah'm so
hail-pliss," she minced. "I don't threaten, I weep in dark
bedrooms and wear out chastity belts. You should have
seen me in the prosecutor's office. I had on one of Helen's
churchy dresses, a dark blue number in honor of the honor
I could have lost." She lit the cigarette and dropped the
match into an empty beer can on the table. "It's protective
coloration. Armor."

"You cut your hair."

She nodded, her short tresses brushing her cheeks. "I
had a bad dream. A guy got hold of it from behind and
wouldn't let go." She smiled weakly. "Couldn't see the
fucker's face."

"He have a big sombrero and a Zapata slash?"

"Black stallion and a silver saddle," she picked up the
joke to counter her blush. "You know, stuff he'd checked
out from props on the studio lot. His old lady sells hog-
brain tacos to the tourists and turns a trick for college boys
now and then."

She eased down into a chair and smoked in silence.
Curiosity left unsatisfied for ten days prompted me to be nosy.

"Mind talking about it?"

She tilted her head back, closed her eyes and exhaled deeply. I watched the rise and fall of her breasts a moment before realizing she was wearing a bra. "I was asleep. A sound woke me up. I got the pistol and went to the work-room door. Somebody was out there, I could see that much. By the wall. I said, 'Who is it?' Whoever it was started mumbling and muttering. Really *borracho*, man. It freaked me. While I was fumbling around trying to get the safety off, he started toward me. When I heard him say *puta* I pulled the trigger." She opened her eyes. "I wasn't trying to hit him, you know? I was shooting at the god-damn ground!" she said with disgust.

"Where's your pistola?"

"I gave it back to Jaime."

"That's good."

She shrugged. "Maybe."

After a moment, she rose. I walked her to the car. She opened the door and hoisted herself wearily into the dri-ver's eat, letting me push the door to.

"You ok?"

"Yeah." She grinned wryly. "I guess I'm just feeling some of the bruises stupid people get before they smarten up." She gripped the wheel and looked ahead, her profile a still life of a driver; when she spoke, her words might have been a voice-over on driving footage. "You can bet your sweet ass I'll never fall in love again!"

She sounded more glad to have been there than deter-mined not to return. Suddenly I was very sorry to see her leave — with some of her sharp edges blunted by experi-ence, she was someone I'd like to know better. Why hadn't I tried?

She was sorry for what she'd done, I for what I hadn't. Of the two regrets, hers was respectable. I patted her forearm.

"Take care, Vera."

"You too."

As she drove away, I saw that the bus had a new layer of dust; inscribed on the rear panel was that ubiquitous plea, *Lávame*! But only I had come full circle; Vera's experience spiralled toward the future, and she was ahead of where she had begun. As long as I was too prudent to be foolish, I never would be wise.

Tether

*A*s James wheeled down the sandy drive, Clara was standing on her porch in a sleeveless knee-length jumper the color of lemon Jell-O. The garment's amusing familiarity made her seem less likely to condemn him; she'd been civil, but distant, when he called hours ago to arrange to pick up his children.

He parked behind her faded green Rambler, noting its license sticker had expired. When he stepped from the carport, she watched with her hand cocked like a bill over her eyes, and he felt as if he were being observed through the wrong end of a telescope. He stuffed in his shirt-tail and gave his watch an overblown scrutiny. James and his kids faced a four-hour drive to Dallas, where he and his new wife, Sharon, were to entertain a filmmaker looking for a writer on a documentary about Arabian horses. James knew nothing about Arabian horses but could feign an expertise with a practiced flair.

He halted at the foot of the redwood steps leading to the porch.

"Hello, Clara."

Her glasses had slipped to the end of her sweating nose, and the chunky lenses magnified her watery blue eyes. The distance in her telephone voice had migrated, like a cold, into her gaze.

"Oh, hello."

"Kids okay?"

"Oh, fine." Her eyes probed his face, then she gingerly rehooked the temple wires over her ears. "These glasses," she murmured.

Two years ago he'd divorced her daughter; he hadn't seen Clara since before then. She still parted her short white hair in the middle so that it eaved over her square head like a hip roof, but lines had radiated outward from a hidden center of her face like rock damage on windshield glass. The jumper hung like a sack. Janice had told him months ago that Clara sometimes "forgot to eat" now that Alvin was gone. James presumed grief to be the reason, but Janice said she was afraid it meant Alzheimer's. On hearing this, James had then sent Clara a card to sympathize with her "not feeling well," as if the illness were a temporary discomfort.

"Lake down?" he asked to draw her out. He, Janice, and the children use to check the water level at the back of the lot on arriving for vacations. When Clara didn't immediately answer, James felt hypocritical for trying to exploit the old ritual for its useful nostalgia.

"Maybe," Clara said finally. She came down past him and headed for the carport. He followed, puzzled, walking along her late husband's dust-covered Dodge and through a breezeway. At the back boundary of the property, she stepped onto a small dock that jutted over a weedy beach. She sat on a bench and stared toward the lake, her head turned away as James mounted the stairs behind her. Heat shimmered over the still water. Far offshore, a Sunfish lay becalmed; the sailors' laughter drifted to them and punctuated their own uneasy silence. James rested one knee on the bench as if to use it like a wooden leg. A good many nails he'd originally driven into the pine needed pounding down again. During summers, when lake water was released through Buchanan Dam to be used by rice farmers far down the Colorado, he and the kids scratched the exposed beach for shards of flint worked by Comanches.

He couldn't stand the silence. "Water's down. Kids find any arrowheads?" He spoke to a skirt of white hair. Her nape had the pale look of an animal's underbelly. Protruding through her huaraches, her big-toe nails looked as thick and yellow as old piano keys.

Had she heard him? He couldn't tell if her remoteness was a symptom or a sign of anger. He'd be truly sorry to have lost her good opinion. She'd climbed out of the potato fields outside Fredericksburg and coaxed her parents to send her to school, carrying her shoes there so they wouldn't look used. She'd been the only one of nine children to graduate from college, had gone alone to Saltillo to teach during the Mexican Revolution. Details of her early life — she and her sisters had had to make their own brassieres from swatches of old sheeting — could've come from a pioneer's story. Befriended by her, he had felt close to history, approved by its superior moral character.

His watch showed 2:30. Already Sharon would be in the kitchen preparing her company casserole and picturing him on the road in her mind's eye.

"Well," James said slowly, "I guess I'll gather up the kiddos." He was prepared to use his prospective client as a reason to bolt but suddenly didn't have the heart for making the excuse. Before he could push off from the bench, Clara turned, grabbed one of his hands, and clutched his index finger like an infant. Her face glistened with tears. In fifteen years he'd never seen her weep; for an instant, he imagined she'd plea for him to go back to Janice, and, shocked, he jerked his finger free.

"Oh, James! I've had one of my spells!"

She covered her face with her hands and cried. Stunned, James dropped onto the bench. He slipped an arm about her shoulders and hugged her, ashamed to have imputed attitudes to her which were actually symptoms of a disease. He had no idea her condition would degenerate so quickly. It certainly explained the vagueness with which she'd greeted him: she simply hadn't recognized him.

After a moment, she caught her breath, and he handed her his handkerchief.

"Did you forget where you were?"

She sighed. "I went to the cemetery but I couldn't go in."

"Oh." She'd been referring not to a failing memory but to her grief. Although her husband had died hardly more than a year ago, it seemed ancient history to James.

"I know it must be hard."

His voice sounded hollow. It was just like Alvin to haunt this woman. A few yards away, a clump of willows grew in shallow water; Alvin's ghost hovered nearby, hip waders over his black wingtips, tie tossed over his shoulder, casting into weeds with a bass lure. It was a perfect expression of his character that he'd fish only where it wasn't possible to catch anything and where you were guaranteed to lose your lure. And do it wearing a necktie because a former parishioner might drop by unannounced. As a semi-invalid, Alvin drove daily to a cafe in Burnet to drink coffee with the natives. Seeing signs of strength in him, Clara would plan to visit old friends in the Valley — she'd been waiting to travel after dutifully serving as a minister's wife for forty years — but when she mentioned it Alvin would take to bed. Clara would arrange for people to check on him while she was gone, but he'd protest that he could care for himself. He'd also declare that the grass needed to be cut, planting in Clara's mind his pushing the old hand mower on an August afternoon, hatless. He'd brought on his first heart attack that way.

Clara was looking at the lake. The water was so still and metallic it gave the illusion it might support weight.

"Are you okay?" James asked, testing her.

She gave him a lucid look, then readjusted her glasses with an air of tidying her emotions. "I go along all right for a while, James, and then it just slips up on me and I have to spill it out."

"It's all right."

"I pray and pray, but there's just such a void."

That was unsettling. Her faith had always seemed quaintly corny, and when black thunderstorms whipped over the lake, sending zags of lighting crackling overhead, Clara's audible murmurs had made him grateful someone wasn't too proud to ask for safety.

He took her hand as they strolled through the yard. He felt curiously light, as if pumped full of helium. The ankle-high St. Augustine had shot runners into the weedy flower bed, and she hadn't pruned her pear tree. Her tomato plants crawled in their plot, leaves curled from thirst. These signs of neglect struck him clearly now, as if he had been the one in a fog. If he hadn't stalled his arrival from fear of an unpleasant reception, he could've mown the grass, pruned the tree, staked and tied the tomatoes, repounded the nails on the dock.

She stopped to admire blooming gallardias. "They've hung on longer than any year I can remember. It seems like everything is trying hard to be cheerful."

"I'm glad you can still think that."

"Oh, I read the signs out of habit." She dropped his hand and passed him the damp handkerchief that had been wadded in her free fist. She lifted a hose from a dike around a Jerusalem fig tree and moved it to another. No water ran from the hose, and the soil under both trees was a jigsaw puzzle of cracked mud scum.

While Clara walked on, James hung back. One tree was pregnant with plump, ripe figs. Impulsively, he stuffed one into his mouth; he chewed the soft, sticky bag of pulp with a furtive haste that baffled him, swallowing as he trailed her toward the house. By the patio, he opened a faucet to run water through the hose to the fig tree. But then he immediately turned it off. It might run for days.

Scattered on a picnic table were bread crusts, Ding Dong wrappers, and two glasses with dregs of a red liquid attracting yellowjackets and flies. Clara always had a passion for cleanliness, and you wiped up your leavings to keep insects away. His children had left blue flippers, diving masks and wet tennis shoes lying under the table.

He squinted through the sliding screen door into the den. On the old Stromberg-Carlson, George Jefferson was shouting much too loudly, his skin the green of Oxydol boxes. The tops of Robert's and Tricia's blonde heads protruded over the back of the couch, unmoving. Had they been sitting there crosslegged like meditating gurus since Wednesday, three days ago, when Janice had dropped them off? Clara used to have them help her bake cookies or hose down the patio. She had taught them to clean fish, play dominoes, and knit, how to tolerate neighbors with uncivilized eccentricities and how to defer gratification by saving trading stamps.

In his most authoritative voice, James bellowed, "This is God speaking!"

Both kids jumped; Tricia turned and squinted toward the window.

"Oh, Daddy." She sounded groggy and cross, as if he were keeping her from sleep. The back of Robert's hand arced lazily in a greeting.

"My first commandment is to clean up your mess out here!" he boomed, but impersonating God hung a piece of phlegm in his throat that made his eyes water. He coughed, then added in his own gravelly tenor so they'd take him seriously, "You guys know better than this."

When he stepped inside, he added, "We're late already, so get shaking!"

The clock above the fireplace had stopped at 6:45 for some other day. It had to be wound once a week. His watch showed 2:55. They should already be in Burnet and turning north on 281 for home.

In the kitchen, the plaster of Paris sculpture of praying hands stood in its usual place on the refrigerator top. Clara's late mother had made it as a crafts project in her nursing home. Painted bronze, it rose on a base formed about the wrists. The way it had always created the startling trompe d'oeil of someone bursting forth from inside the appliance like a Jack-in-the-box usually made James smirk, but now the hands belonged to a quicksand victim.

A Tupperware pitcher of cherry Kool-Aid stood inside the refrigerator, surrounded by bruised and jay-pecked peaches. James poured some into a plastic glass, swallowed it to sluice the fig seeds from his teeth, rinsed the glass and upended it in the drainer. Picking up the Comet from the counter, he started to sprinkle cleanser into the greasy sink, but set the container down instead. A clock ticked loudly in his head. One project would only bait him into another until he was caught and reeled in.

A saucepan over a burner showed an inch of charred material glued to its bottom. Clara had forgotten to turn off the burner. She might do that then doze off. Was there a smoke alarm? And if so, was the battery good?

When he went into the dining room, Clara was seated at the formica-topped table. A large purse of brown vinyl that looked like a grocery sack with a drawstring sat before her.

"James, help me to concentrate, will you? I've lost my. . ." She frowned, trying to recall either the thing or the name for it.

"What's it used for?" he asked, as if she had posed a riddle.

"My driver's license," she sighed. "I've looked all over." From the purse she took a checkbook wallet with a credit card folder which she unaccordioned for his inspection. One window held a snapshot of Robert and Tricia, another her social security card, but the rest were empty.

"See, it's not where I usually keep it. I went to town yesterday."

Robert entered carrying the two glasses from the picnic table, passed behind James and into the kitchen.

"The day before, Grandma," the boy called over his shoulder. The plastic glasses went thunk into the sink. James wanted to tell him to wash them but let it pass.

"Was it?" Clara craned her head to see into the kitchen. "Were you with me?"

Robert leaned against the door frame and raised one dirty bare foot to scratch the shin of his other leg.

"No, ma'm. Don't you remember, Grandma? You went by yourself, then you forgot where you were going. Your friend Jean found you and drove you home."

Robert passed James a look that said telling more would embarrass his grandmother. "You were there all afternoon." James had a sickening vision of Clara wandering around Burnet in a daze. Looking at her wallet, he noticed that the checkbook was not in its customary slot, either. Was it missing, too? He hesitated to ask. The more he dug, the more he might uncover.

"I've got it down in my diary." Clara went off, presumably to fetch the diary. Losing his driver's license and checkbook would have panicked James, and his pulse quickened to consider it. She needed their help, and he hated to desert her. But the items might be found in five minutes or five hours, and already Sharon was most likely setting places around a centerpiece of day lillies. He had to stop on the way home to buy wine.

Several minutes later, Clara returned with a black book the size of an accountant's ledger. She reseated herself, opened the book with an air of expectation, and studied it.

"I didn't write down about going to the dress shop." She removed her glasses and, head bowed, pinched the bridge of her nose, concentrating. Or praying. James shifted his weight from foot to foot, standing at the table.

"You went to a dress shop while you were in town the day before yesterday?" A call to the shop might solve the mystery.

She squinted into the diary. "What's the date today?"

James checked his watch. "June 26th." It also read 3:30. He'd have to chance a speeding ticket now.

"Oh my," she murmured. "I guess I got a little behind." She grinned impishly to permit him to laugh at her, but he didn't.

"Did you go to the dress shop before or after you went to the cemetery?"

"I just don't remember, James," she said, as if it were

normal to forget. Which was, James considered, precisely the case. "I guess I should call Jean."

"You called her already, Grandma," Robert said. He had plopped onto the living-room sofa with an Incredible Hulk comic, feet resting on a stuffed Adidas dufflebag. James wondered if he'd made his bed. "She said you didn't have the driver's license in the dress shop when you went in to buy something."

"Maybe I left it in the car." Clara rose quickly, walked into the hallway, then James heard a sliding screen door scrape open and shut. He jumped up from the table and hurried into the living room. Tricia was holding a pink zippered bag full of clothes in one hand; clutched under her arm were two Barbies.

"You kids help us, okay?"

"Dad! We've been looking ever since we came!" wailed Tricia.

He strode through the bedroom they'd used and observed that they'd pulled their quilts into a position approximating "made," then went out to the carport.

Clara sat in Alvin's old blue Dodge, squinting at a map spread over the steering wheel. The sight of her there, glasses at the end of her nose, brought him to a halt. She looked so frail, so pitiful and lost that the Arabian horses seemed as remote and unimportant as the region of their origin.

Was she thinking of driving to see her daughter in California? Now that Alvin was gone, she was "free" to travel. She might get as far as San Angelo before forgetting her destination, even who she was. She was free to get lost in all that space in the West, drift rudderless and without an internal compass into her own Horse Latitudes. There'd be no Jean out there to reroute her.

And who could stop her? Her son, Walter, was stationed

in Germany. Her oldest daughter hadn't returned from California to attend her father's funeral, so her mother's lapses in memory wouldn't inspire a visit. That left Janice, who, like James, lived 225 miles away, and she was busy carving out a new career in furniture brokering. And what could or should James do about it? Insist to Walter and Janice that Clara be put in a nursing home? Clara would have to be a babbling idiot before she'd agree to leave the only home she'd ever owned after living in parsonages for four decades. No, the pot on the lighted burner would send the place up in flames before that. His heart turned slowly over to consider her inevitable future.

He moved to the driver's window.

"You find the license and the checkbook?"

"Oh, am I missing the checkbook, too? Oh, dear!"

It took her a good while to refold the road map, but not much longer than it would've taken him, had he bothered to do it properly. She did it with excuriating leisure, as if pleased to solve this puzzle, at least. Meanwhile, James tried to construct a probable itinerary for the Wednesday past: first to the cemetery, where she'd become disoriented from grief and had the onset of a "spell," on to the dress shop and to some other place(s) where she'd left the missing items, then to wherever she'd been discovered by Jean.

"Did you go to any place besides the dress shop?"

"I don't remember, James. I'm sorry." She emerged from the car with a frown. "Maybe I put it down in my diary."

Exasperated, James followed her to the dining table, where she picked up her diary, gave it a cursory glance, then said, "No, my diary's not up to date. I need to do that."

"Where were you when Jean found you?" An aspect of this mystery that required a detective's logic was faintly enjoyable to him.

"I wish I could remember. I guess I could call Jean."

"You were at the grocery store, Grandma," Robert tossed in from the adjoining room.

It irritated James that Robert tuned in as he pleased and dropped little chunks of reality into their confusion with lofty condescension.

"Well, if you were at the grocery — "

"You'd think someone would have called by now," Clara finished quickly for James. Her swift deduction reassured him.

"Did you have groceries with you when Jean found you?"

"It wouldn't necessarily mean anything. I pay cash for them, too. But, anyway, I was empty-handed. I mean except for this purse."

"It'd be a good idea to call the bank about the check-book," James said after a moment. Some such decisive act might give him a wedge for departing. "Usually you need to close out your old account so nobody can write checks on it."

She nodded, then drew a red Bic pen and an envelope from the purse. She wrote in large letters that had the wild parabolas of carnival rides. Call bank tomorrow, James read upside down.

"You'll have to wait until Monday. Banks are closed tomorrow." He looked away from her. Surely the note or her memory of it would be lost by Monday. As well as one to buy a smoke alarm. Or batteries. Or to wind the clock, turn off the burners, water the trees.

"Of course," she said, a trifle lightly.

He risked wounding her pride again by adding, a little hopelessly, "You'll need to know your account number when you call. Maybe you have it on a cancelled check. They won't do much over the phone without it."

On the same envelope, Clara wrote *get account number* so laboriously James wanted to scream.

"Maybe you should report the loss of your license, too," he went on, despite a silent vow to let all of this rest.

"They told her to order another one," piped in Robert.

"Wait!" Clara held up her palm as if to stop traffic. She riffled the diary's pages and stopped at the last entry. Nothing in the diary would help, he knew; he could feel the sun sinking in the western sky, the earth wheeling under them while they all moved as if mired in molasses.

"I went to the cemetery on the anniversary of Alvin's death, the 13th," she spoke crisply. "This last entry is for the twelfth."

Her "spell" had lasted not a few hours on Wednesday or today, but, rather, for the past fourteen days, James calculated with an inward sigh. It was why she had quit writing in the diary; the license and checkbook could have vanished any time over the past two weeks.

"That's my problem, you see." Clara's eyes were filmed with tears but her voice remained firm. "I keep forgetting that Alvin died, but then I just remember it all over again."

"Lord," James muttered. No doubt it was Alvin she'd been expecting as James drove up. He looked out of the window at the lake silvered like a mirror in the heated stillness, seeping away from its banks too slowly to notice. As macabre as it sounded, should he post Alvin's obituary on the wall? Clara could surely remember he'd died, then, and eventually be able to forget it. Maybe she'd agree to a housekeeper who could keep her oriented on the present.

Clara went to a wrought-iron telephone stand, slid open a drawer, and extracted a piece of paper, which she proudly held up to show.

"I've got it all written down here. I've already called the bank and taken care of it." She gripped one lens like a monocle while she read. "I called last Monday and talked to a Mrs. Johnson."

She set the paper on the table, weighting it with a salt shaker. Walking into the living room, she picked up her knitting from her Sears swivel rocker, sat down and began to untangle the yarn. The finished product trailing from the needles was an amorphous swatch. Her needles clicked softly as she worked them intently only millimeters from her nose, the way she'd peered at the map. A curious absorption in her posture froze his heart. It was as if her reward for finding the paper that settled the matter was to slip back into that world where Alvin was still alive.

"She found that yesterday, too." Robert put down the comic and sat upright on the couch, feet on the floor, a miniature adult. Now did James see what they'd been up against?

"Clara."

She stopped knitting to peer at him. He was relieved that she seemed alert.

"You need to keep the diary up to date. I know it's hard. I've got one myself, and everybody has to help me remember what went on the day before." It was true, and he could all too easily imagine himself in her condition. "It's probably a good idea of keep your notes and lists centralized in the diary so they won't get lost."

Clara chuckled. "Well, of course, I have to keep track of the diary, too."

"I know," said Robert. "Let's put it on a string the way you do pencils and stuff."

"Good idea, son!" James clapped Robert on the back, strode into the kitchen, took an ice pick out of a drawer, and brought it back to the boy. He doubted the idea would help much but thought it would make the kids feel better, at least. It might keep Clara connected until he could see to doing something more.

Together, the kids punched a hole in the diary, then Robert tied one end of some twine through it and knotted the other to a spindly leg of the telephone stand. While they watched, waiting for her approval, Clara gave a perfunctory tug on the cord, much too gently to test the knots truly, and told them it was fine.

Plane

*J*ames lay awake planning a letter to Dear Abby. *My
son is bringing an expensive gift to my birthday party
tomorrow night, and I suspect it was bought with ill-
gotten gains. Do I accept it?* This version had been
whittled down from many paragraphs; "ill-gotten
gains" still had a Victorian stink.

Margaret said, out of the darkness, "I wish I could help
you settle your mind about it."

"Me, too. It's like a Cleaver problem only in this episode
the Beaver is a felon and Ward and June are divorced." Ill-
gotten gains was vague, anyway.

"Officially you don't know anything."

James sighed. "We're not talking legal, Margaret."

Richard had called Margaret mid-week to report he'd

bought James "something really awesome" but wouldn't
say what. Margaret told Richard that James might feel
uneasy about taking such a gift from a poor student. "Oh, I
got money," he said. "Don't worry about it." When the
boy dropped out of college, James had stopped his
allowance, and, rather than live with his mother or James
and work, he had been free-loading with friends. He had
no job, but, according to his mother, Richard was running
a pyramid scheme; he preyed on rich kids he'd met in the
dorm.

"He's proud of this present," Margaret warned James.

"Obviously, or he wouldn't have called you."

Margaret drifted off. Three doors down, the cocktail
waitress who lived with a postman slammed her car door,
and James followed the tick-tock of her heels down her
walk. Son, I'd rather you gave me a McDonald's gift certificate earned by waiting tables than anything bought by con-
ning somebody. The bigger the present, the worse it is. You
want to give me a present? Show me one ounce of honesty,
integrity, or grit.

Video games. The kid had been fantastic, lightning
reflexes. Initials burned into the blanks of the top ten. One
good semester in drama, another later in art. This against a
hundred thousand hours of air guitar, sky-larking, drugs,
elaborate but feeble lies. Am I to blame?

Mid-morning, James called Richard's mother.

"I think I've decided what to do about this present. To
spare his feelings, I'm going to take it and act like he made
the money by the sweat of his brow, but I think I'm going
to give it to the Salvation Army. I don't want to have to
explain to a court how I took it knowing that it had been
bought by bad money."

"It will crush him," Richard's mother said calmly.

"Christ, I'm not going to tell him."

"He'll know if you're not using it."

"You know what it is?"

"Yes. But he asked me not to tell."

"Oh, get serious!"

"Really. I promised."

For a moment, James wanted the gift. After all, it was his birthday, and this dilemma had already ruined whatever pleasure might have been in it.

"Do you think it's right for me to take it? Would you take it?"

"He thinks of himself as an entrepreneur."

"The law says different. And you didn't answer my question."

"It's very important to him what you think of him, James."

"Thanks for nothing."

James had planned to spend this Saturday afternoon reading some science fiction. Instead, he went to his garage workshop. Spread on a long wooden table were the parts to a model B-25. Blueprints were thumbtacked to the wall behind it. The flourescent fixture coughed up a cold light as James pulled a stool to the table. The completed fuselage lay like a huge insect husk amidst a jumble of ribs and pins and templates. The wings lay apart in skeletal form, their spars still uncovered, looking like the weathered bones of a bird. He stared at the arrayed parts for a minute before discovering where he'd left off weeks ago. Left rudder. These weren't hard to build, but it took patience. It taught patience. He'd built dozens of simpler models as a kid, balsa wood cut from a pattern then glued together and pinned to the board to dry. Old-fashioned — not your pre-fab plastic model a moron could slap together in five minutes. He unscrewed the cap on the glue, smelled it, and the sharp odor took him back. He never heard of getting high on it then; now kids inhaled a smorgasbord of household products that seared their tissue and short-circuited their nervous systems. The poor kids. White kids like Richard did Ecstasy, coke.

James had started the B-25 right when he and Richard's mother were divorced a decade ago. He'd pictured himself and Richard side by side on matching stools, James passing on the tips, the lore, the kid learning patience and the satisfaction of completing a labor of love. He'd thought they'd have a fine time flying the damn thing. What happened? I want to watch my shows, Dad. Sitting two feet from the screen, his face bathed in that lurid light. Later it was roller-skating, next thing you know he was up all night in the clubs, stoned, dancing.

Margaret brought him a mug of hot tea. "I need vanilla and candles for the cake. I thought maybe you'd like to get out."

"I'm not brooding."

"This is the brooding place."

"Yes. But it's my birthday."

"And I'll cry if I want to?"

James laughed. "Well, yes."

"Look," said Margaret. "If you think you and Richard are going to fight, please tell me now. I hate to go to all the trouble of making this dinner thinking my guests will wind up throwing it at one another."

"I don't want to fight. I want to be able to accept him and what he gives me."

"So do it."

"It's hard. I'm disappointed in him."

"Be patient. Give him a chance to grow up."

Off to the store, James felt unfairly accused of rigidity. To him, it wasn't right to ignore Richard's behavior if it were criminal; furthermore, it was dangerous to Richard for them to do that. Both Richard's mother and Margaret were tender-hearted when they should be tough. Because no one had ever demanded of Richard that he do anything hard, he'd gotten no training in it. Other things came too easy: Richard had looped both women into his confidence and thus into an alliance. Now he could give his present knowing James had heard about it, yet since James didn't "know," he couldn't openly accuse Richard of buying it with dirty money. These were neat maneuvers; no wonder Richard was enjoying success as a confidence man.

The Sunkist cornucopia, festive bins of nuts — strolling the color-dappled aisles of the supermarket under the rain of merry Musak hiked his spirits an inch or two. He saw Richard's eager, boyish face, the gift-wrapped package presented, then the moment of dread when both giver and receiver hold their breaths, each longing to be pleased, each fearing disappointment and rejection. Was it okay just to unwrap it, smile, keep his mouth shut? Wouldn't it encourage the kid to buy a gift twice as costly next time? When he was three or four he'd bring home things made for his parents; once it was a pinched clay dinosaur that looked like a dog turd, and James had said, "Thank you, son! Good boy!" The gift was good, the praise was good — they were parents encouraging a child in giving. Either that same principle applied here years later or this was a pathological mutant of it that should be exterminated.

James handed the grocery sack to Margaret. "You know what I hate? That I'll never be able to use it without knowing where it came from."

"Oh, maybe after a while what seems like a big issue will just fade away."

"I wish that idea was comforting."

"It happens sometimes."

"Oh, I didn't say it wasn't true."

James was on his second glass of Beaujolais and had just put Ladysmith Black Mombazo on his tape deck when Lou arrived, ten minutes early. She was carrying a bottle of Blue Nun and something round covered in Christmas wrap that James knew would be a Mason jar of peaches from her backyard tree. They'd helped her put them up last summer. Although usually seen in overalls, this evening she was wearing lipstick and black bell-bottom slacks.

In the kitchen, Lou gave Margaret the bottle of Blue Nun.

"Can I help?"

"No thanks, I got it," said Margaret, passing the bottle on to James.

"Okay if we stick to red?"

"I'm not insulted."

James opened a new bottle of Beaujolais and poured three glasses. They stood within arm's reach in the kitchen, the bare-bones nucleus of a party. Then Margaret set her glass on the counter and weaved herself in and around them as she made salad.

"What's that music?"

"African," said James. "It's an album called 'Journey of Dreams.'"

They both postured as listeners a moment. Lou was a devotee of Lawrence Welk reruns. "Too churchy," she said. "Frank liked that ranchero music." She sipped her wine. "Well, you're still a youngster."

"I guess."

"Oh puh — shaw. I was your age, me and Frank still took ten-mile hikes and had relations twice a week."

James and Margaret laughed. Lou, pleased with herself, blushed. "No, I mean it. A person young as you can still look ahead and make a different future."

"I suppose," said James.

"Oh, I am full of it!" laughed Lou, watching him.

James heard the front door open, then the Newbys walked into the kitchen, Sally leading, pushing a wave of Halston ahead of her, Roger's head bobbing over her shoulder. She hugged James and kissed his mouth, her breasts pressing against his ribs.

James herded his guests into the living room and took orders: Sally, red wine; Roger, vodka on the rocks with a lime twist, Lou a glass of her Blue Nun. Returning to the kitchen, James felt faintly annoyed. He wanted to be waited on hand and foot for this occasion.

"Richard's going to be late as usual," he told Margaret as he was pulling the vodka bottle from the freezer.

"Spaghetti will hold. That's why I planned it."

"Smart of you."

"You do like it, you know."

"Yes, but it would be nice to choose."

"He's a kid."

"He's nineteen." James heard his voice rising.

"I was married to my high school sweetheart, that's how dumb I was."

James laughed. "Okay. But thirty minutes is all. Beyond that, he can sit in the corner and eat alone."

Margaret smiled. "Too bad he wouldn't think of that as punishment."

"I know."

In the living room, Lou was telling the Newbys that her daughter, a divorcée with two children, had been fired from the state driver's license bureau, where she'd worked for ten years. "She says it wasn't her fault, but, you know, she never could get along with people. She can be the most hateful person I ever knew," Lou said cheerfully. "I'm surprised she lasted as long as she did. I told her not to come crying on my shoulder."

"So it never ends," James said.

"What?" Lou asked.

James shrugged, suddenly uneasy.

"Being a parent," put in Sally.

"I don't see how. Why would you want it to? It keeps life interesting."

They laughed. James checked his watch. Richard was thirty-two minutes late. James was about to suggest to Margaret that they eat when he saw Richard pulling to the curb behind the wheel of some other child's BMW. James knew the exact cost of such a car but had ridden in one only twice.

Richard came up the walk carrying a box wrapped in silver foil in one hand. He was wearing black loafers with no socks, black wool slacks, a white dress shirt and red tie (silk and Italian, James later noted), and a heavy gray Cosby-show cardigan. Watching through the window, James estimated the cost of Richard's outfit at about $600, roughly a week of James's salary.

"Happy Birthday, Dad!" Richard burst through the door, grinning. When Richard thrust the box into his hands, he immediately set it down on the coffee table. He and Richard A-frame hugged.

"We were about to give up on you, boy!"

Richard laughed. "Yeah, I'm late, nothing new. Hi, Mr. Roger! Mrs. Sally! Lou!" They stood, and Richard worked them like a crowd, pumping Roger's hand, hugging the women. The foil on the box reflected back a sunbeam. Everyone smiled. They were enveloped in a cloud of Richard's cologne. It was hard to stay mad at him.

"So how's Paige?" Richard asked the Newbys when all were seated.

"She's doing fine," said Sally. The Newbys' youngest daughter had been a classmate of Richard's; before adoles-

cence the two offspring had been close, but as teenagers
they had little contact. Richard called her a student council
twit.

"She's — ?" asked Richard, though James suspected the
boy knew the answer.

"At Rice."

"On scholarship," put in James, then regretted it. "At
least I think so. Isn't that right?"

"Yes," murmured Sally. "She's home for the weekend.
She may drop by."

"You want a beer, son?"

Richard grinned. "In lieu of a scholarship?"

James shrugged. "Whatever. How's your drink, Roger?"

"One more of these and I'll be cross-eyed."

In the kitchen, James fixed vodka and lime for himself
and Roger. To Margaret, he said, "Richard's here now."

Margaret set the salad bowl down hard on the counter.

"Yes. I heard."

"I'll try to cork it."

"Promise?"

During dinner, Richard raconteured, acting out a story
about a big black dude working on the street in front of his
friend's apartment. One day when they pulled into the
driveway he approached the boys to ask if they needed a
bodyguard to escort them to the Prince concert. You white
boys be all right with me. Two hunnerd dollars. Nobody
mess wit you! In Richard's anecdote, the worker sounded
like Mr. T. The boy was a good mimic, and they laughed,
but shadows of interpretation fell across the content. The
black man, laboring in the street, sweating, sees the white
kids step from the BMW; they hear him out, then waltz
giggling into the condo supplied by someone's mother.
Another story concerned a boss who had fired Richard.
The lively enactment of a key scene had Roger slapping the

table with laughter, but the subtext nagged at James. The boy seemed in such a good mood; James realized it was built on the illusion that he was about to give a gift that would stun his father into approving of him.

"Your Dad tells me you're planning to go back to school next semester," said Roger.

"Yeah?" Richard looked surprised then gave his plate a little moué of disgust. "Maybe. Who knows?"

"What would you like to study?" asked Sally.

"Economics maybe."

James smiled. At four Richard had wanted to be "a policeman or a bird."

"This generation," Roger chuckled. "I once told Paige that her mother and I had thought about becoming missionaries and she acted like we must have been crazy."

"That's because she'd never seen us go to church."

"Well, they're lucky they can still be whatever they want," said Lou.

"What'd you want to be when you grew up, Dad?"

James was startled. "Oh, well, gosh! A casualty claims examiner, what else?"

They laughed.

"Come on, Dad, really!"

"It's true. Even as a toddler I dreamed of an office the size of a gymnasium, a platoon of gray desks, me there with yellow pencils and one of those green shade deals, eagle-eyeing other people's pathetic little swindles."

Roger raised his glass. "Let's drink a toast to middle-age melancholy."

"Let's don't," said Margaret.

"It's for young people, anyway," said Lou.

"Thanks, Dad."

"I'm sorry. It's been so long I don't remember."

"Are we ready for dessert?" asked Margaret.

Richard wriggled like a five-year-old in his chair while James lingered over his cake. After Margaret cleared the table, Richard jumped up and retrieved the foil-wrapped package and set it on the table along with Lou's present and a package the Newbys had brought.

James didn't want to torture the boy, but he dreaded opening Richard's present, so he took Lou's first. The peaches turned out to be a small bottle of good cognac. The Newbys had brought a tape of the Gipsy Kings and a book of paper airplanes.

Steeling himself, James took Richard's foil-covered gift and unwrapped it. A jewelry box. He opened it and blinked. In his mind's eye he saw the point of his yellow pencil. Taken in burglary. Men's TAG-Heuer quartz diver's watch. Rotating bezel, sweep second hand, chronograph, alarm. In stainless steel. $750, he'd guess.

"Wow!" said Sally.

"I'll say," said Roger.

Richard seemed to be holding his breath. James passed the box to Margaret to inspect.

"So, Dad — you like it?"

"Well!" James looked at Margaret; she kept her eyes on the watch and gave him no cue. "It's very costly, son. This will take some getting used to."

"Try it on for the wrist size."

Feeling trapped, James took the watch from Margaret. It was deliciously weighty, the finely machined dials suggesting the serious, infallible precision of aircraft gauges. He admired the way it looked; even if he had an extra $700, it would be hard to spend it on himself, and he longed to keep it. He unsnapped his $30 Citizen, laid it aside, then he slipped his hand through the gift watch's expansion band; it felt tight like a cuff on his wrist and the watch was heavy when he raised his arm to gesture.

For the next hour or so, he wore it but tried to ignore it. Lou and Richard sat in the porch swing smoking Lou's Raleighs; Paige showed up to wish James a happy birthday, a little puffy-jawed ("freshman fifteen," she said, though he made no comment) and looking tired. To James's surprise, Paige took Lou's seat when Lou left, and she and Richard switched to Paige's Marlboro Lights, chatted quite aimably for half an hour, and kissed when Paige left. They were like mock grown-ups.

Once when no one was observing, James slipped into the bathroom to inspect the watch. It looked new; therefore, it hadn't been stolen. In a house burglary, anyway. He frowned, glaring at it as if expecting the answer to the uninvited dilemma it had posed to be found on its face. Its luxurious, costly look made it clear he couldn't avoid grilling Richard about how the watch had been purchased. He dreaded it. Richard had absolutely beamed as James unwrapped the gift. Already there was the scholarship remark, and the flip answer about his childhood ambitions. When you grow up, Dad. Why hadn't he given a better answer? Did he have one? Once he thought it would be great fun to work in South America constructing clever bridges out of indigenous materials. What did it feel like to be young enough that a whiff of perfume and a girl pressed to your side meant possibility?

When everyone had gone but Richard, James handed him a beer the boy had not asked for and said, "Son, I'm a little bothered about something."

Richard grinned. "I know. You're worried about how I paid for that watch."

James's heart skipped a beat. "Yes."

"Well, in the first place I didn't have to pay full price."

"How's that?" Counterfeit, James thought.

"A guy I know works at a place that sells them and he gets a discount."

James presumed this was a lie. "That's good. But even so, it must have cost a lot. It worries me that you spent this much because you don't have a job."

Richard kept grinning, as if he had a great surprise for James. "You think I've been dealing drugs or something?"

"I don't know. I only know you haven't been working."

"No, you only know that I haven't had an employer."

James assumed a baffled look to hide his sinking heart. Out of the corner of his eye, he saw Margaret pass through the dining room, glance toward them, and continue on quickly.

"I have been working."

"What have you been doing?"

"I'll show you." Richard jumped up, went out the door and ran down the walk to the BMW, the gray wings of the cardigan filling with air. James turned away from the window. Richard returned after a moment with a large black ledger, went to his knees at the coffee table, opened the book and spread it before him.

"This — I've been working on this." Across two pages like a girly magazine centerfold had been drawn the skeletal cross-section of an airliner. James thought of Wonder Woman's translucent plane, with its undulant, curving fuselage outlined in electric yellow. In the nose of Richard's was a black label — "Pilot" — with "Richard" penciled beside it. Other labels carried out the metaphor — Co-Pilot, Navigator, Passengers. Some labels had names, others were blank.

"What is it?"

"It's a money machine! It's great. I've got six of these going right now. You can get in on it if you want. What you do is this. You sign on as a passenger and you buy a ticket. Then — "

"How much are the tickets?" James instantly perceived the scheme to be a variation of a chain letter.

"Two hundred. It goes to the pilot. As each new passenger comes on and buys a ticket, you move up in the cabin closer to being the pilot, and — "

"Richard, this is illegal."

"Only if you don't report the money to the IRS."

"I don't know who told you that, but it's wrong. This is a pyramid scheme, and it's illegal because there are no goods or services exchanged and because if you work them out mathematically, pretty soon everybody on the planet would have to be involved, and all those who come on last get cheated."

"I'm not going to be last, Dad. I'm the pilot."

"I didn't mean you'd have to worry about being cheated. I meant you'd have to worry about cheating somebody."

Richard's hurt look said *Just like I expected,* and James realized too late that this ingenious scheme was more than a means of getting the present; it was to have been a gift, too.

"You don't understand it."

"No, *you* don't understand it."

"Dad, I've got lawyers and doctors and architects on some of those other planes. I have to work at it."

"The Reagan administration had cheats and thieves and liars in every other office, but that doesn't mean you or I have to be those."

"Like you never broke any law in your life, right?" Richard slapped the book shut, stood and jammed it under his arm. "Like you and Margaret don't haul out the old hash pipe now and then." His chin was trembling. "Like you've spent your whole life being an upright citizen."

James stood; they faced each other over the coffee table. The boy was taller than James; his nostrils were flaring, but he looked as if he might cry.

"Don't drag out the old divorce crap, Richard."

"Yeah, I know it never meant much to you."

James groaned. "Oh, come off it, Richard. That's ten years old."

"It's fresh in my mind. Must be nice to have your memory."

"And it must be nice to have something so convenient to blame any time you fuck up."

Richard shifted his weight to his other foot. Wit flashed behind the boy's eyes, his lips curved into a grin, and he said, "I call it the designated excuse."

They both smiled.

James stretched across the table and awkwardly laid his palm on Richard's shoulder.

"Look. It's just I worry, you know? Jail isn't a nice place."

"Don't worry."

"Don't do things that cause me to worry."

James walked his son out to the BMW. Richard got behind the wheel, and James stood at the window for a moment, admiring the deep black paint on the car.

"Nothing but the best. Right?"

"Piece of shit, Dad," scoffed Richard. "It's falling apart."

"Let's hope it doesn't disintegrate while you're driving it. I imagine the parts come pretty high."

"Don't worry, Dad. Robert's mom'll take care of it."

Margaret had been watching them from the livingroom window.

"So?"

James grinned; he felt oddly elated, buoyant. "So we're both alive."

"What about the watch?"

"Oh, Christ! I forgot about it." His arm flew up; he'd

gotten accustomed to the weight. He took the watch off his wrist. "I don't know."

Hours later the watch awakened him. It made a strange, insistent peep, like an electronic chick. He got up and looked for the sound, stumbling in the dark, until he remembered setting the watch on top of his dresser. He groped for it, grasped it, and it kept peeping in his hand. He carried it into the bathroom, where, squinting against the blinding overhead light, he worked to silence the alarm.

Witnesses

Norma should tell this story, but I don't think she will. So I have to do my best, though I might not tell it exactly as it happened. My story is this. Norma called me to say that her friend Patsy had died. I'd met Patsy once when she'd come to Dallas to collaborate with Norma on a book about quilting.

I told Norma I was sorry to hear about Patsy. "I know you must be devastated," I said. "You were friends for such a long time."

Yes, said Norma. "Since we were twelve." They'd grown up in New Mexico together, got married and divorced in tandem, stayed cross-continental pen pals for forty years. Patsy, childless, was godmother to Norma's daughter.

Was it cancer?

"Her heart exploded," said Norma.

You know Patsy, she went on, how she kept really fit and ran three miles a day —

It was like Jim Fixx? No warning at all?

"Well, she'd had a leaky heart." A congenital condition. The doctors had told her she was at risk in jogging, "but she wanted to take care of her problem this way." And she'd been doing fine.

It happened while she was running?

No, it was like this. Patsy was coming out of a supermarket. She was carrying a bag of groceries in her arms. A woman walking into the store happened to look at Patsy's face and saw her eyes roll back. She realized Patsy was passing out, so she stepped right up to Patsy and hugged her. The woman struggled to hold Patsy upright until a second woman, then a third, saw what was needed and rushed over to help the first woman lay Patsy back onto the floor. The second woman took off her gray cardigan, folded it, and slipped it under Patsy's head. While the third retrieved cans of cat food that had spilled from Patsy's sack, the first woman told a checker to call an ambulance. She pressed her fingers to Patsy's wrist but didn't feel a pulse. A fourth woman with wild red hair and paint-dabbed jeans went to her knees, loosened Patsy's concho belt, then blew into her mouth, over and over, and massaged her chest. Meanwhile, the second woman looked into Patsy's purse and located her home phone number, but when she went and called it, of course all she got was Patsy's machine. With nothing left to do, the other three knelt beside the woman doing CPR and waited.

The paramedics arrived but couldn't bring Patsy back. When they had put her on a stretcher and slid her into the ambulance, the first woman took out a business card, wrote on the back of it, and slipped it inside Patsy's purse, which the red-haired woman was holding. She in turn put the purse into the ambulance, and the third woman sat the groceries by Patsy's side.

The first woman's name is April Yuan, and she is a buyer for an import firm. When the ambulance left, she and the other three women stood at the curb for a minute, not knowing what to do. April Yuan had gone into the store to buy pantyhose because she had a 2:30 meeting, and it was already 3:00. The second woman draped her gray cardigan over her forearm and stroked it as you might a cat.

The other woman who had helped lay Patsy back, who had retrieved Patsy's cat food and had put Patsy's groceries in the ambulance, said, "Well, I've got to go back to work now. It's a day-care center, couple blocks up that way." She looked to April Yuan and the others as if for permission to leave, and they shrugged and murmured that they understood. But then the day-care worker, a care-giver, made no move to go. The woman with the cardigan said, "I'm just visiting Berkeley, and I don't know anyone here." The woman who had tried CPR said, "I need to sit down and have some tea." The visitor with the cardigan looked relieved and said, "Me too."

They all four walked down the street a way until they came to a cafe none had ever been inside. The tables were of plywood with glossy, lacquered tops, and the menu said, we serve no caffeinated beverages. April Yuan, who has since been back to the place twice with Rachel, said the lunch crowd had cleared out. The place was quiet and empty but for one waitress who was wiping tables with a natural sponge the size of a bread loaf.

The four women ordered orange-cinnamon tea. The waitress brought a teapot with a blue glaze and four matching mugs on a tray. Then after a moment the waitress brought, unasked, fresh hot blueberry muffins for them to sample free. They didn't talk much at first. The red-haired woman lifted her mug high enough to peer at the bottom of it. Somebody said, "Poor woman." The visitor's hands were trembling, so her tea got cold before she could drink it. The red-haired woman said this was the only time she'd ever used her CPR training, and the others said don't feel bad — it was good that you tried, it was more than we did. The woman who worked at the day-care center asked, "I wonder if she had children?" April Yuan had noticed Patsy had no wedding ring.

They stayed for about an hour. The funny thing was, said April Yuan later, "We didn't talk about your friend Patsy very long." They didn't know what to say about what had happened. They all talked for a while about being parents and having them. The visitor with the cardigan said she had two teenage sons back home in Michigan. April Yuan has a grown daughter, but she told the others only about her mother, who has Alzheimer's. Then the visitor from Michigan asked the day-care woman how she put her hair in those corn rows. It takes days, answered the other. You got to wait until you want to punish yourself. They all laughed. They talked about the tea, the crockery. After a bit, April Yuan got up to go call her husband even though she knew he was busy at work, and when she came back to the table, the others were standing over the bill and chatting while they dug change out of their purses and pockets.

April was the last to leave the cafe. The woman with the teenage sons was already striding far up the street. A breeze had come up while they were in the cafe, and, while walking, the woman slipped her cardigan over her shoulders. Beside her, the day-care worker was gesturing in a way that meant giving directions. When the two reached the corner, they both looked back and waved good-bye. Then they disappeared.

The red-haired woman in the paint-smeared jeans had been lagging behind, letting the other two outpace her. She stopped and waited for April to catch up to her. "I'm Rachel," she said, and stuck out her hand. "I saw what you wrote on that card about being with her when she died. I hope someone from the family calls you."